The Wild One

By:

Brooke St. James

No part of this book may be used or reproduced in any form or by any means without prior written permission of the author.

Copyright © 2022

Brooke St. James

Other titles available from Brooke St. James:

Another Shot:
(A Modern-Day Ruth and Boaz Story)

When Lightning Strikes

Something of a Storm (All in Good Time #1)
Someone Someday (All in Good Time #2)

Finally My Forever (Meant for Me #1)
Finally My Heart's Desire (Meant for Me #2)
Finally My Happy Ending (Meant for Me #3)

Shot by Cupid's Arrow

Dreams of Us

Meet Me in Myrtle Beach (Hunt Family #1)
Kiss Me in Carolina (Hunt Family #2)
California's Calling (Hunt Family #3)
Back to the Beach (Hunt Family #4)
It's About Time (Hunt Family #5)

Loved Bayou (Martin Family #1)
Dear California (Martin Family #2)
My One Regret (Martin Family #3)
Broken and Beautiful (Martin Family #4)
Back to the Bayou (Martin Family #5)

Almost Christmas

JFK to Dublin (Shower & Shelter Artist Collective #1)
Not Your Average Joe (Shower & Shelter Artist Collective #2)
So Much for Boundaries (Shower & Shelter Artist Collective #3)
Suddenly Starstruck (Shower & Shelter Artist Collective #4)
Love Stung (Shower & Shelter Artist Collective #5)
My American Angel (Shower & Shelter Artist Collective #6)

Summer of '65 (Bishop Family #1)
Jesse's Girl (Bishop Family #2)
Maybe Memphis (Bishop Family #3)
So Happy Together (Bishop Family #4)
My Little Gypsy (Bishop Family #5)
Malibu by Moonlight (Bishop Family #6)
The Harder They Fall (Bishop Family #7)
Come Friday (Bishop Family #8)
Something Lovely (Bishop Family #9)

So This is Love (Miami Stories #1)
All In (Miami Stories #2)
Something Precious (Miami Stories #3)

The Suite Life (The Family Stone #1)
Feels Like Forever (The Family Stone #2)
Treat You Better (The Family Stone #3)
The Sweetheart of Summer Street (The Family Stone #4)
Out of Nowhere (The Family Stone #5)

Delicate Balance (Blair Brothers #1)
Cherished (Blair Brothers #2)
The Whole Story (Blair Brothers #3)
Dream Chaser (Blair Brothers #4)

Kiss & Tell (Novella) (Tanner Family #0)
Mischief & Mayhem (Tanner Family #1
Reckless & Wild (Tanner Family #2)
Heart & Soul (Tanner Family #3)
Me & Mister Everything (Tanner Family #4)
Through & Through (Tanner Family #5)
Lost & Found (Tanner Family #6)
Sparks & Embers (Tanner Family #7)
Young & Wild (Tanner Family #8)

Easy Does It (Bank Street Stories #1)
The Trouble with Crushes (Bank Street Stories #2)
A King for Christmas (Novella) (A Bank Street Christmas)
Diamonds Are Forever (Bank Street Stories #3)
Secret Rooms and Stolen Kisses (Bank Street Stories #4)
Feels Like Home (Bank Street Stories #5)
Just Like Romeo and Juliet (Bank Street Stories #6)
See You in Seattle (Bank Street Stories #7)
The Sweetest Thing (Bank Street Stories #8)
Back to Bank Street (Bank Street Stories #9)

Split Decision (How to Tame a Heartbreaker #1)
B-Side (How to Tame a Heartbreaker #2)

Cole for Christmas

Somewhere in Seattle (Alexander Family #1)
Wildest Dream (Alexander Family #2)
About to Fall (Alexander Family #3)

Hope for the Best (Morgan Family #1)
Full Circle (Morgan Family #2)
Just for Tonight (Morgan Family #3)

Chapter 1

Rose Cameron
***

Broken Arrow, Arkansas
Late December
A few years ago

The man of my dreams had broken his shoulder right in front of me in a devastating skateboarding accident. He got up after it happened and said he was fine, but I had seen it happen, and the memory of it still haunted me. We weren't sure if it was broken, but Eric was injured, and I had watched the crash take place. His girlfriend hadn't even seen it. She was looking away. But I saw the skateboard come out from under him, and watched him fall, and now I was emotional from it.

Maybe I was being emotional about other things. As aforementioned, the man of my dreams has a girlfriend, after all, and he has no idea that I even had any dreams about him. He was now and had always been oblivious to me. Maybe that was the real reason I was so emotional. I was invisible to Eric Jones. I always had been. I had known him since we were kids. I was older than Eric by more than two years, which seemed like an eternity back then.

We saw each other once or twice a year when we were young, and then my family stopped traveling to Arkansas after my grandmother died. At that point, my grandfather went to live with my uncle in Houston, and we didn't visit the lake house anymore.

Now my uncle owned that house, and again, our extended family began to meet up in Arkansas whenever possible. I loved going there with my family, and one of the reasons was that Eric Jones lived nearby.

I reconnected with Eric recently because his dad got a job as the groundskeeper for my uncle at the lake house. My uncle did not live there full-time, and it was an estate with a main house and multiple other buildings, so it needed full-time maintenance. Also, Uncle Max's son, my cousin from Florida, had recently fallen in love with and married Eric's sister, Hope. So, their family would be around every time I came to Arkansas now. It would have been glorious, but unfortunately, Eric was taken and living in Nashville.

We were all at the lake house now, though. My whole family was staying here for Christmas and the wedding. There were aunts, uncles, and cousins, and even still, Uncle Max had room for more.

Even though the house was amazing, Eric was still the best thing about Broken Arrow. He had grown up to be funny and worldly, and now that we were older, it felt more appropriate to be attracted to him.

But I had lost my chance. He was all grown up and living in a different state. He was in a serious relationship with a woman named Jillian. She was there, in Arkansas, with him now. She was beautiful and nice, and I hated her good-for-nothing guts. I didn't really hate her. I couldn't. I had no reason to hate her, other than the fact that she had Eric and I wished I did.

I had never met anyone else like Eric, though. He was fun and fearless. He knew how to juggle and skateboard really well, and he could play a few different instruments and sing. He told stories and jokes. He was the life of the party type, but he also had manners and was considerate. Not to mention, his face. Eric Jones's face was a thing of great beauty. He had a gorgeous, wide, full-lipped smile and piercing blue eyes. He had immaculate hygiene and was always clean and smelled nice, but he also carried himself like a rockstar. He had long-ish shaggy hair and he gave off that vibe that he didn't care what anyone else thought of him.

Eric had an easygoing attitude, but he was a hard worker and he tried his best at things. This was apparent when I watched him skateboard. He was so good that it was captivating. He knew a ton of tricks, and I watched him perform them, knowing that he had practiced each of them thousands of times in order to master them. My two brothers and all of my cousins were all athletes and hyper-competitive with each other, and none of them came close to Eric on a skateboard. He was legitimately talented, which was incredibly attractive when I realized how difficult that skill was to learn.

Eric Jones was also the most handsome, intriguing guy I had ever known. And now that we were old enough for me to do something about it, he was unavailable.

I normally wasn't the type to get emotional and start feeling helpless about men that would never be mine, but I had just witnessed my cousin getting married, and right then, I felt hopeless about love. Plus, I had watched Eric get physically hurt and could do nothing to help him because it wasn't my place. He and Jillian had gone to Little Rock to get an X-ray, and I was left feeling lonelier and more hopeless than ever.

"What are you doing in here in the dark?"

My mother's voice cut through the silence, and it startled me.

"Mom. Please. I'm sleeping."

"Why are you in bed at this time of the afternoon, Rose?"

"I'm taking a nap."

"You never take naps. You only take naps if you're sick. Are you sick?"

"No, I'm not sick, Mom. Please don't come in. I don't want to talk right now. Please let me rest."

"Why are you… have you been… are you *crying*?" She asked the question in a tone that said she thought it was an impossibility.

"No," I lied.

"What's going on, Rose?" She began crossing the room, and headed for my bedside.

"Mom, I'd really like to get some rest. Please."

Astrid Morgan, my lovely mother, was a famous ballerina turned ballet instructor. She and my father had been happily married my entire life, but she kept the last name Morgan while the rest of us took my father's last name, Cameron. My extended family that got together in Arkansas were all Morgans. It was my cousin, Charlie Morgan, who got married to Eric's sister this weekend.

I was never a dancer, but my mother used that same pull-no-punches, tough-love approach with her children as she did with her students. It didn't surprise me that she continued to come into the room despite my wishes. I turned over, facing away from her, and moaning, pretending to be asleep even though I wasn't.

"Rose. Look at me. I can tell you're crying. What's going on?"

"I didn't like seeing Eric get hurt," I said. "I watched the fall. I saw him land on his shoulder. He landed right on it. I think he hit his face. I'm just worried for him."

She sat on the edge of my bed and leaned over, turning on my lamp.

I squinted at her. "What are you doing?"

"Rose Cameron, you are a straight-A student. You've taken enough biology classes over the years to know the human body. You've seen your brothers fall, get hit, and break bones your whole life. Surely you don't mean to tell me that you're lying here with a wet pillow and puffy red eyes from seeing some guy, some degenerate, fall on a skateboard." Her tone was one of utter disgust.

"Don't call him that," I said, turning to look straight at my mother.

She leaned back, making a surprised expression. "So, the tears are more about the guy than the fact that someone got hurt."

"Mom, please stop." I turned my pillow over and took a deep breath. I faced away from her again, but she didn't move. We stayed there for what must have been a full minute.

"That guy is not worth it," she said, finally, at my back.

"Thanks," I said. I was being sarcastic.

"No, I mean he's *actually* not worth it," she said. "I know I could say he's not worth it just to make you feel better, but I'm not doing that. He's actually not worth your time, Rose. I have *no idea* what you see in him."

"Everything. I see everything in him. I like every single thing about him."

"He literally has nothing to offer, Rose. He's some hotshot skateboarder? That means nothing. He has no plans to do anything with his life. He moved to Nashville and moved in with a girl. He didn't go to college. He's a skateboarder. You would never forgive yourself if you tried to go after a skateboarder with no plans and settle for that. His dad works here, for goodness sake. He's probably going to end up doing something like this with his life. No offense to Mr. Paul, because he's a nice guy, but you don't want to marry that. He's got a tiny little one-bedroom place. How would he have a family in there?"

"I never said I was going to marry anybody, Mom."

"Well, then there should be no tears. The only man important enough in your life to cause tears should be the one you love and the one you're going to marry."

My mom's matter-of-fact statement made me smile humorlessly. The funny thing was that she thought her reasoning would solve everything. She imagined that I would turn off my tears like a faucet, paste on a smile, and go on about my day, realizing that Eric was never worth it in the first place.

"Thanks for judging him, Mom, but it already wasn't going to work out between us before you said any of that. He's living with that girl, and—"

"Exactly. He's living with a girl. You can stop there. That's all you needed to say. I can't believe you're even thinking about him in this way, shedding tears, after you say that. Think about it, Rose, at this very moment this man is headed to a hospital because he is so irresponsible with his own health that he falls off of a skateboard. Maybe he's handsome, but, believe me, with your résumé, and your family, and all you have going for you, Rose, you can get someone that is both handsome *and* stable. You do not need to live your life with somebody like that. Don't base your decisions on looks or the fact that he can juggle and flip a skateboard. Nobody's going to care about that stuff in ten years when you guys are calling us up asking for money because you can't get by."

"Thanks, mom. I'll try to remember not to call you up and ask you for any money in ten years."

"That's not the point I'm trying to make, Rose. The point is these tears are all in vain. He is not worth it, which is exactly what I said at the beginning of this conversation. We could've skipped this explanation. He is not worth it, and that's all that should've been said. We've all seen them making out in the gazebo all weekend."

"Mom, please," I pleaded as I felt a stab of pain in my heart. "I haven't seen that."

"Well, I have," she said. "And I do not want my daughter's mouth being in the same place that all those other women hav—"

"Thank you, Mom," I said again, cutting her off since I could bear to hear no more.

"Seriously, though, Rose. You are a grown woman. You've been to college, and you have a grown-up job."

"I take notes and make appointments. I get coffee for someone else with a grown-up job."

"You know what I mean. Your job is leading to something. You've been to college, and you have a future."

"I've been to school with plenty of people who will do nothing with their life, Mom, and Eric hasn't been to school, but he will do something with his."

"Well, right now he is at a hospital with a broken shoulder from riding on a skateboard. And he's there with someone else."

"You said that already."

"Well, it's something that needs to be repeated until you figure out that I'm right."

"I'm not saying you're not right, but that doesn't make my heart hurt any less."

"It should. If you know he's not the one for you, then just mentally move on. You are strong enough to do that, Rose. You have had to mentally move on from things in your life. We're women. This is not your first tear-stained pillow, and it won't be your last. Just make up your mind to get through this trip without letting it affect you. They will go on and live their life and have drinking problems and failed marriages and whatever it is that unprincipled people do. You have a different path to take, and even though it might hurt a little right now, just tell yourself that the destination is so much better and so worth it."

"I didn't know he was bringing her, or that they were going to be staying here."

"I know," she said, shaking her head. "I don't know why Uncle Max let them stay here when his mom lives nearby. But it's his house. I guess he can do whatever he wants with it."

"Eric is Hope's brother, so technically, he's related to Uncle Max now, right?"

"I don't think so," Mom said. "Now that I know he's done this to you, I think it's kind of obnoxious that they're here. I can tell Uncle Max, and he'll have them stay at Eric's mom's place."

"Eric hasn't done anything to me, Mom. I just like him. That's no reason to punish him."

"I don't want him around if he's causing you to end up like this."

"Can't I just have a minute alone to be emotional? I'm not ending up like anything. I'll smile and go on and have Christmas, like always. I just watched him fall, and then I watched her treat him like it was no big deal before they left. She didn't see it happen. She doesn't know how hard he fell."

"You need to lay here for a few minutes until you realize that none of that is any of your business. Skateboarders fall all the time. There's probably a skateboarder on some stairs falling and breaking a bone right now—several of them. None of that is any of our business. It's a waste of time thinking about it. I'm not surprised you have a heart for him, though, Rose. Do you remember when you were twelve years old and you tried to get his dad a raise? You made a whole chart of everything he did for grandpa. That's just your mentality. You have a heart for working-class people. I can see why you like that boy, but you need to get past your emotions and know that none of this has anything to do with you or your future. Give yourself one hour to let all of this sink in. Lie here and cry for a minute if you need to, but then think about everything I said and realize that I'm right. You are truly better off without that boy. I would not want someone like him as my son-in-law, Rose. You don't want to start a relationship with someone if your mom's saying that about them. Think about those things, and your heart will feel better about all this."

Chapter 2

Broken Arrow, Arkansas
A year-and-a-half later
Summer

I had been in Arkansas for most of the summer. I didn't plan for that to happen, but I was in between jobs, and my family was spending some time there, so I took a few weeks off before starting my new job.

Eric Jones was back in town, but again, there was nothing between us. He had just left Nashville to move back home. He looked great, but he had come back to Arkansas with not much to his name. He had stories and life experiences but nothing material to show for the last few years, and no job prospects. Since he had come home, he had picked up work with his dad working for my uncle. He was a hard worker and I respected him, but he was starting over here in Broken Arrow—there were no two ways about it. He had a car that wasn't too dependable and he was living with his parents, going back and forth between my uncle's house and his mother's place which was thirty minutes away in a neighboring lakeside town named Graham's Ferry.

Eric was still a wonderful guy, but he had focused on having life experiences and he didn't have much in the way of material possessions or professional prospects. This was in stark contrast to Charles, the guy I had been dating for the last four months. Charles had a great job as an engineer and a gorgeous apartment in Chicago.

Granted, nearly half of our relationship had been long-distance since I had been at the lake house most of the summer. But I was technically dating someone back home in Chicago, and therefore Eric and I were just friends.

We had spent a lot of time together this summer since he was working at the house, but neither of us had any problems hanging out and maintaining a casual friendship—we had been doing that since we were kids. I loved to hang out with him.

Chicago was cold, and we were bound to the indoors during the winter, so roller skating was a popular pasttime. I had bought myself a nice pair of roller skates months ago before I ever started dating Charles. I decided to take them to the lake house with me this summer, and I was glad I had because Eric had taught me a lot and given me good advice. I was far better at skating now than I was when I first came to this house, and I owed Eric for that.

We had spent hours together while I practiced roller skating. Sometimes, he would skateboard, and sometimes, he would watch me and give me advice. He didn't know anything about roller skating and, sadly, the moves didn't translate, but he had a good knowledge of body physics, and he looked up tutorial videos and coached me.

I was still as physically attracted to Eric as ever, but I wasn't prone to cheating and I didn't let myself see him that way. I simply turned off my attraction. I wasn't superficial enough to let my mom talk me into losing feelings because he was poor, either. That didn't matter to me.

He was back in Arkansas, starting over, but it wasn't his financial situation that made me lose feelings for him. It was that he had a life these past years. He had a serious relationship where he lived with a woman.

I gave up on Eric before I ever started seeing Charles. I liked Eric a lot as a friend, still, though, and we didn't hesitate to spend time together. We were spending time together at this exact moment. I had suited up in my roller skating gear and was with him in the garage.

As a beginning skater, all of my time was spent on flat ground. Eric rode on inclines, rails, stairs, and anything else you could think of, but not me. I was a the-flatter-the-better girl when it came to my skating surfaces. I liked them as flat and smooth as possible.

I was currently working on a move called the dribble. It was a basic roller skating dance move—one of several where a person's feet fluidly move beneath them while their body stays stationary.

"My body's not staying stationaryyyy!" I warned in a helpless tone as I drifted backward, toward Eric and began to lose control. I waved my arms in a circular motion to try to give myself forward momentum, but I couldn't reverse the action. I couldn't stop drifting.

Eric came up behind me and caught me just as I started to pick up speed. He smiled as he gave me a little push, sending me gently the other way.

I sighed, feeling defeated. "I am not getting any better at this," I said. "It's the hardest one. How is it basic?"

"Don't stress about it. Your body will understand it eventually. Just work on other stuff if you're frustrated with dribbling. Drill those step-overs, or do some backward bubbles. I'll put on some music."

I sighed again at the thought of going backward. I had fallen three times doing that lately. I had fallen down enough that I now wore wrist braces when I skated. How I could manage to fall when I was going about zero miles per hour was beyond me, but it was totally possible.

"Don't be defeated," he said. "You have to put in the work if you want to get better."

"I'm leaving tomorrow. I've been at it for weeks, and I still can't do these dribbles."

"You're a lot better than you were when you first started."

I smiled. I felt like he was wrong, but I wasn't going to pout. "You're right," I said, even though I didn't quite believe it. I took a deep breath and stood up straight in a resolute pose.

Eric tilted his head at me. "Why do you want to learn how to skate, anyway?"

He asked the question slowly and he gazed into my eyes. I wondered, as he stared at me, if he thought that it had something to do with him. My heart started beating faster, and I swallowed, realizing that maybe I wished he was thinking that.

I looked away and cleared my throat.

"My boyfriend goes to the gym a lot," I said. "But regular gyms aren't really my thing. I've never had fun lifting weights or taking classes. Anyway, there's this skating rink close to where I'm going to be working when I start my new job, and I went to check it out before I came here. They sold me these," I said, pointing at my feet.

"They're awesome," he said. "I don't know anything about skates, but they look nice on you. I like the suede."

"Yeah, I paid way too much for them. They put specialized wheels on them—and some other parts, too. Plugs. Is that a thing? I think that's where the breaks used to be."

He shrugged. "I have no idea. It's not like that with a skateboard."

"Anyway, there are parts on here that are custom. I'm trying to be like these people who jam-skate. Did you know that was such a thing before we started doing these drills?"

"No," he said. "I've seen people at skate parks on skates, but they don't do that."

"Yeah, this stuff is popular in Chicago—at skating rinks and stuff. They make it look so easy."

"You'll make it look easy eventually. You're already a lot sturdier than you were."

"Thank you for the vote of confidence. I feel like I'm not even able to work on any moves yet. I'm still learning how to stand up on these things."

"That's what you're supposed to be doing right now," he said. "If you could learn it all on the first day it wouldn't be fun anymore, would it?"

"I don't guess so," I said, smiling at him. "Speaking of fun, that's another reason why I do it."

"Why?" he asked.

"My mother. She's always been really strict and proper and expected me to behave like a proper lady." I smiled at him and shrugged. "And most of the time, I do just that. But, something about skating seems, I don't know, rebellious. It's not rebellious, technically, which is wonderful. I get to feel like a rebel without actually breaking any rules."

"It feels rebellious because it's so hard," he said.

"What?"

"You have to basically hurt yourself a ton to get good at it," he explained.

"Is that why it's rebellious?" I asked, taking a second to think about it.

"I don't know. I made that up. But probably. It's true, you do have to hurt yourself some in the process. You fall. And there are times when there's going to seem like no growth. Believe me, I know how that feels. It's hard to keep trying when you fall a lot or hit a plateau in practice."

"I can't imagine you ever not being good at skating," I said. "Even when you hurt your shoulder that time, it was because you were doing that crazy flip thing. I can't imagine you falling like I fall where I'm just suddenly off-balance for no reason. I don't even hit a rock, and I just suddenly start falling."

He laughed. "Oh, ask Landon how many times I've fallen," he said, talking about his best friend. "I've fallen way more than you. I fell yesterday."

"Yeah, show me that thing you were doing yesterday. That one where you twirl it around your foot."

"The Casper flip?"

I nodded, and Eric leaned over and retrieved his skateboard, which was propped against a wall.

I smiled as I heard the familiar sound of it clacking on the concrete near his feet. Eric stepped onto it like a pro. He was smooth and steady on it, and I watched as he skated out of the open garage door and down the slight slope onto the driveway, picking up speed. He continued skating to an open area and then I watched as he flipped the skateboard in a most unusual manner and then smoothly landed the trick. He bent his knees, absorbing the shock when he landed, and then he began heading back toward me, smiling.

"I can't even tell what you're doing! It twirled around your foot."

Eric came into the garage, stopping and kicking up his skateboard in a practiced movement.

"You're funny. You said you couldn't tell what I was doing, and then you told me exactly what I was doing. That's all it is, twirling it around your front foot."

"So much easier said than done," I said.

"Yes, you're right. That one took me a while."

"Well, you're amazing at it now," I said.

"Thank you. I might only have three hundred dollars to my name, but at least I can land a Casper flip."

"Three hundred isn't bad," I said. "Most people are in debt."

"Oh, I'm in debt, too," he said. "I have a few grand in credit card debt, and my truck's not quite paid for." He smiled "So, I guess I don't have three hundred dollars, after all."

I shrugged. "The only reason I'm not in debt is because my parents helped me through college and bought my car. If I had student loans and had to buy a car, I'd be in a ton of debt right now."

I sat on a nearby ledge and concentrated on taking my skates off. I leaned over, untying and loosening the laces.

"I'm going through with that business," he said after a few seconds.

"Building decks?" I asked, not looking up at him.

"Yes. I like it, and I'm good at it. My brain works that way—basic building is easy and fun for me, and people around here are always needing decks and docks built. I figure if I do a good job and do it right, I can build up a reputation and eventually make a business. Landon is going to make me a logo."

"That's awesome. And, you're right, you can build a reputation. If you like building decks, you can do it for a business. Especially around here. Personality is part of it, and you have that part down already, so now you just have to get really good at building. Do you think you like it enough to do it day in and day out?"

"Yes, I do. I mean, eventually, I'd want to be the guy who makes bids and manages jobs, but I don't mind the labor for right now."

"I think you should go for it," I said.

Chapter 3

Later that evening, I stood in the kitchen with several others. My cousin, Casey, was in for the weekend. It was his dad, Max, who owned the lake house, and Casey and Max were a lot alike. They both got along well with Eric, which was why Max had hired him to work since he'd been back in town, and why we were all in the kitchen talking.

Uncle Max and Casey asked me about my new job, and I told them I was headed back the following day to start it. Casey had just arrived and had been out of the loop.

"I know it's a jewelry manufacturer, but what exactly are you doing?" he asked. "I thought you were a writer."

"I did graduate in journalism, and technically, the job I just left at the newspaper seemed like a better place for me to work. But I spent over two years getting coffee and lunch for my boss. I thought I would be able to build relationships with him and have the people at the newspaper respect me eventually, but that..." I trailed off shaking my head. Eric had been hanging out with me all summer and had heard me say this whole bit a few times.

"That didn't happen?" Casey asked, finishing my sentence.

"No, it didn't happen," I said. "They didn't want to build a relationship with me. They just wanted me to get coffee and mind my own business." I shrugged. "I understand, but I had to move on, for my own good."

"I thought Aunt Astrid said you did get a job writing somewhere."

"I will be writing… a little. I'm working for a jewelry company, describing their catalog. I also have to compose emails and revise company publications. It's not a newspaper, but at least I'll be writing something. It's definitely not my dream job but ironically, it'll be better than the newspaper, which is where I thought I wanted to work."

"She's got to get back to the glory days of Rose Knows," Uncle Max said.

Eric looked at me curiously, and I shook my head. I had spent the summer with Eric, and we had talked about a lot of things, but I had intentionally left this information out. My column in the college newspaper had been extremely popular. I was part of a sorority, and I had two brothers, Beau and AJ, who were local athletes who played division one lacrosse at Notre Dame. My parents were both sort of famous and had a ton of connections. I knew a lot of people in Chicago, and I knew how to be in the loop on my campus.

I started the 'Rose Knows' section as a joke to tell my friends what our options were for the weekend. One thing led to another and my column became a hit at my university. Even as I was there, and the whole thing was still going on, I knew that it couldn't last forever. I graduated and had to move on and get a real job. There is still a similar column at school, only it has a different name.

I pitched the Rose Knows column to my boss at the newspaper during my first month, and he laughed. He brushed me off. I wasn't trying to hide that information from Eric, but I didn't mention the column because I was currently doing something that was less interesting.

"I used to have a section in the college newspaper," I said to him since I could tell he was curious. "It was called Rose Knows, and I gave advice on where to go and what to do. It was like a community events section."

"They should have given you a better job right out of the gates for making a successful section like that," Max said, being a protective uncle.

"Thank you," I said. "I wish it worked that way. But I'll get there. I'll find something I like doing, and then I'll be nice to the people getting me coffee one day." I shrugged. "Maybe I won't by then. Maybe I will have had to deal with so much crud to work my way up that I'll be just as jaded and mean as the rest of them once I'm there."

"You'll never be like that," Eric said. His tone was certain, and I turned to stare at him. Those unbelievable ice-blue eyes. They got me every time. They were a light grey color with darker blue around the edges. I had never seen eyes like them in my entire life. I did my best not to stare into them, because I had always gotten butterflies over the years when I looked directly into them.

I needed the excuse to look away so I headed for my phone. A minute earlier, I heard vibrating from over on the counter where it was sitting. It was quiet, but I knew where my phone was, so I was aware of the subtle sound. It went off for a long time—long enough that I knew someone was calling multiple times.

"I need to check on something," I said. I walked to the other side of the kitchen where I found my phone on the counter. There were four missed calls from Charles.

"Hey, I have to deal with a phone call," I said to all of them. I took off, heading out of the kitchen, calling Charles as I walked. No one could hear me by the time he answered.

"What are you doing?" he said. "I tried to call ten times."

"I know. Why would you do that?"

"Because you didn't answer," he said.

"You don't have to call that many times. I didn't have my phone. What's the matter?"

"My mom. She's reserving our places at that concert. Dinner will be served. She needs to know if you want steak, chicken, or fish."

I let out a sigh. "That's why you called four times? I thought it was an emergency."

"She needs to know, Rose, and I don't want to take a guess at it and be wrong. It's three hundred dollars a plate. I don't want to get there and have chicken and you look at me and say, 'where's my steak'."

"I hope you know me well enough to know that I would not say 'where's my steak', Charles."

"You know what I mean. She's reserving the tickets, and she needs to know."

"Isn't there something else we can do with three hundred dollars besides have a chicken dinner?"

"No."

"Okay, well, then, chicken. I'll officially order the three-hundred-dollar chicken."

I walked into the den and flopped on the couch, continuing my conversation in there since no one was around.

"What are you doing?" Charles asked.

"I was in there hanging out with my family."

"Who's all there?"

"My cousin, Casey, from Florida. I think he was somewhere else before he came here, but he lives in Florida. Anyway, he just got here."

"At least it's not the skateboarder," he said.

"What do you mean?"

"I'm glad you're coming home tomorrow," he said, not answering the question.

"What?"

"I don't like you hanging out with that guy."

"Eric's fine. He's harmless."

"He's going to get you hurt. One time, when I was ten years old, I got a scooter and went to the skate park with it, and these guys talked me into dropping down off the wall with it on day one. They said I should just drop down and they'd catch me if I fell."

"Did you do it?" I asked.

"Yes."

"Did they catch you?"

"Yeah, and they were really nice about it and gave me a gold medal."

"Really?"

"No. I broke my arm in two places. I face-planted and almost died, and those guys laughed at me. They sat on the side and cracked up that I actually did it."

"I'm sorry," I said. "That really happened?"

"Yes."

"I am so sorry. That's terrible. Eric's not like that. He's such a nice guy. He's helping me with all my drills."

"No guy just helps you with drills, Rose. If he's helping you out, he wants something from you."

"He doesn't want anything from me. He just got out of a long relationship where he was living with a woman. Believe me, it's not like that with us."

"Why is he always there? What does he do for a job?"

"He works here. That's why he's always here. We skate after he's finished working. It's no big deal at all. I'm actually going to miss having him around. We don't like each other that way at all. You'd see if you were here."

"I don't know why we're talking about this, anyway. I'm just ready for you to come home. I hope I can talk you out of those skates once you get here. They're dangerous. Just come to the gym with me if you want to get in shape."

"I might do that," I said sweetly, even though I did not mean it.

I liked skating. It was good exercise, and I had fun doing it. I didn't want to be on the phone with Charles anymore. I didn't feel like talking, but I hadn't talked to him all day, and I knew if I tried to get off so quickly, he would overreact and it would result in an even longer conversation. I could not act like I was in a hurry. I had learned the hard way that being in a hurry didn't go over well with Charles. I relaxed on the couch.

"What did you do today?" I asked him.

I thought I heard footsteps, and I listened, but heard nothing. I got up and walked quietly to the door as Charles explained his day's events. I saw Eric in the distance. It had taken me a second to get to the door so there was no way for me to know how long he had been standing there. I tried to rack my brain to think about what he could've possibly overheard. I wondered if I had said his name. I didn't have it on speakerphone, so he hadn't heard the story Charles told about the skate park.

I started to cross to Eric or say something to get his attention, but I just let him walk away. I would be seeing Charles tomorrow, and I knew I owed him a conversation after not checking in with him all day. It had been a few days since I had a good, patient conversation with him, and he would be disappointed if I ended the call so soon.

"Rose?"

"Yeah?"

"Do you have anything to say?"

"About what?"

"I told you my boss chewed me out for something that wasn't my fault and then came back and apologized."

"Oh, that's crazy. I'm sorry."

"Do you remember what he said?"

"What was it?"

"I told you all that a second ago, and you weren't listening."

"I wasn't trying to lose track," I said. "I thought someone was overhearing me, and I walked across the room to check."

I spent the next twenty minutes on the phone with Charles. I tried not to feel jaded about it. I tried to give him the attention I knew he deserved. He just wasn't nearly as easygoing as Eric was, and I had to fight feelings of resentment over it.

I told myself that everything would be fine once I got back to my life in Chicago.

Chapter 4

"Where's Eric?" I asked once I got back into the kitchen a little while later and noticed that he was no longer in there.

"Oh, he went to bed," Uncle Max said. "We're starting early in the morning."

"Is he spending the night here?" I asked, feeling sad that he had gone to bed without telling me goodbye. He knew I was leaving in the morning. It wasn't like him to go to bed so early when we were all hanging out, especially without saying goodnight.

I said a few things to my uncle and cousins about unrelated things, but I couldn't get Eric off of my mind.

"I'm going to try to catch Eric before he falls asleep," I announced nonchalantly. "I probably won't get to tell him goodbye in the morning, so I need to go now."

I told my family where I was going, but I was not asking their permission nor did I hesitate. I said all of that as I was walking out of the room and nobody moved to stop me or really even paid attention to me leaving. I headed through the living room, up the stairs, and down the hallway that led to the room where Eric was staying. He was in the bathroom with the door closed and the light on, and I decided to wait in his room until he was finished.

He had taken over this room somewhat. Technically, he was living with his mom, but he spent most nights here since his mom's house was thirty miles away and they usually started work early. He had a few personal items in the room, but not much for someone who spent so many nights here.

The lake house was basically a palace. There were eight or ten bedrooms in the main house and multiple apartments and guesthouses on the property. Eric's bedroom was one of the more modest bedrooms near the front of the house. It had a bathroom, but it was one of those Jack-and-Jill ones that shared it with the bedroom next to it.

Eric had been in this room quite a bit this summer, but the room had no clutter whatsoever. There were two skateboards propped against the wall. His keys and wallet were neatly positioned on the corner of the dresser. His keychain caught my eye, and in the spirit of wasting time, I went over to look at it. It was an image his friend, Landon, had drawn. It looked like a homemade, one-of-a-kind keychain featuring one of Landon's characters.

I squinted and saw that there was another keychain, a smaller one that said, EJ + JM. The old girlfriend. It was probably something she had given him. My first feeling was to be disgusted and wonder why it was still on there, and then I remembered that it was none of my business. I had a boyfriend. I glanced downward just to pull my eyes away from the offending keychain. *Why were pieces of her still around even though she wasn't?* I felt sick to my stomach about it, and I closed my eyes, begging myself to stop caring.

There was a small trashcan next to his dresser, and it was in my line of vision when I glanced down. There was nothing in it. It had just been cleaned. There was a thin liner, and nothing inside, save one small scrap of paper at the bottom. It was a folded piece of paper that was yellow and looked like a post-it note. I leaned over and peered into the trash can. With the way the paper had landed, I could see some writing. It was Eric's name, and it was in *my* handwriting. It was familiar. My heart pounded as I leaned down and picked it up. The water had stopped running in the bathroom, but there was no way I was going to leave this in the trash.

I took a closer look at it. It was flat and had the slightly tattered edges of something that had been in his wallet for a long time. I saw his name on the outside of it written in my handwriting, and I knew what the note was before I unfolded it. I went ahead and opened it, anyway, and yes, sure enough, there it was, my note to him.

Hope you feel better!

There was a heart at the bottom with my name.
It was from the shoulder incident.

I studied it for a few seconds, wondering why it was in this trashcan. I had just folded it up when I heard the door open.

It was Eric, and he opened the bathroom door, causing light to pierce into the dimly lit room. I had been caught. I didn't have time to throw the note away again. By instinct, I clutched it in my palm and swept it behind my back. "Hey," I said, acting as calm as I could be.

"Hey, what are you doing in here?"

I had on pants with pockets, thank goodness, and I put my hands into them leaving the note in my back pocket.

I took a deep breath as I calculated the scene. Eric didn't look that happy to see me. He gave me a smile, but it was small and guarded.

I was already overthinking things, and I knew I needed to say something. That was almost impossible because he was not properly clothed.

He had on pants but no shirt. I had seen him in the pool this summer, but I had never been this close to him when he was shirtless like this. He was right there in the room next to me. The only light was a lamp, and it was shining gloriously on him, casting shadows on his rows of flat muscular abs.

I made myself look away.

I looked at his eyes.

No.

I stared at the floor.

"I was coming in here to tell you goodnight. And goodbye, since I'm leaving in the morning. I didn't know if you remembered that."

"I remembered," he said. "I thought we said goodbye earlier."

I flinched at his coldness. Eric had never been like this with me. He was always sweet and considerate.

"Did you hear me on the phone?" I asked. The question came out of my mouth before I could even think about what I was saying.

"Yes."

We glanced at each other, and his ice blue eyes stared straight through my soul.

"Is that why you threw away that paper?" I glanced at the trash can as I took a step back.

Eric leaned forward and peered into the trash can. "What paper?"

"The note I wrote," I said.

I took it out of my pocket and held it up, and Eric stepped forward to take it from me. I pulled my arm back as he came forward, and he reached for the paper.

I stretched further than he reached, and he missed. He stopped short, looking at me as he hovered next to me. He had just gotten out of the shower. I could smell the freshly-washed scent on him and feel heat emanating off of him. His bare skin was only inches from me—so close I could feel the heat.

"Give it to me," he said. He stood up straight and held his hand out, looking at me like he knew we could be reasonable. "It's mine," he added. "And what are you doing going through my trash?"

"You had no other trash in there," I said. "I wasn't going through it. I just glanced down and recognized it. It's my handwriting."

We were quiet for way too long.

"So?" he said, finally.

"So, you threw it away."

"Yes."

"Today?"

"Yes."

"Why?"

"Because I didn't want it anymore."

"Why not?"

"Because I was cleaning out my wallet," he said, taking a step back. He didn't bother putting on a shirt. He just stood there and stared at me with a straight face.

"Why is this the only thing you cleaned out of your wallet?" I asked.

He shrugged like it was an irrelevant question. "Because I didn't want it."

"Why did you have it this long?" I asked.

He stood there and kept staring at me. "Because I did want it."

"It's not funny," I said.

"I didn't say it was."

"You're smiling." I stared at him, not knowing what else to say. This was all too much for me to handle. I knew what Eric looked like without a shirt, but I had never been standing right next to him when he was freshly showered and brooding.

"I'll just leave it in the trash," I said.

"Fine. It's just a piece of paper."

"I was coming in here to tell you goodbye, Eric. I'm leaving in the morning, and I know you're working early, so I didn't know if we would—"

"Bye," he said, cutting me off. He reached out to hug me. I went to his arms. He controlled the hug. He took charge and gave me a quick emotionless squeeze before letting me go and stepping back. "Have a great trip," he said.

"Thank you." I stared at him. I wanted to say, *"That's it?"* but instead I just stood there.

"Maybe I'll see you at Christmas," I said.

"Yeah, if I'm still working here."

"Okay, then," I said.

I knew he heard me in the den. I knew that whatever he heard me say had come between us. I felt desperate about it. I couldn't even remember what I had said.

"I don't know what you heard me say on the phone, but I'm sorry, Eric." I felt tears sting my eyes as I spoke, and I blinked, holding them back.

"It's fine. You've got a boyfriend. I understand."

"No, you don't understand because what I have is not the same as what you had. You lived with a woman. I'm just dating a guy. We go out on dates and then he drops me off at my apartment. We barely talk."

"Okay, great, well, I guess you'll see him tomorrow."

"Why are you mad?" He didn't seem that mad but I kind of wanted him to be. I wanted something to happen besides this boring, emotionless goodbye.

"I'm not mad," he said.

I threw the note in the trash and stood up in front of him with a resolute sigh. "Can we please just hug and say a nice farewell and pretend this conversation never happened? I'm sorry for digging through your trash and for whatever I said on the phone. I'm really sorry."

I was looking downward, so it took me by surprise when Eric took me into his arms. He hugged me, oblivious to the fact that he had no shirt. My face was pressed against the warm skin of his neck, and I tried not to notice the feel or smell of him. I hugged him back, telling myself that Eric was like a brother to me and I had no feelings for him. I concentrated on not feeling anything as we hugged, and before I knew it, he was letting me go.

He smiled at me as he stepped away.

"I thought we were going to stay up," I said.

"I'm getting up early," he said. "I have to go to bed."

"Okay," I said, my heart feeling broken.

He pulled a t-shirt out of the drawer. "Goodnight, Rose. I had fun with you this summer. You should stick to skating." he smiled at me after he pulled on the shirt.

"I will," I said. I made a little face at him. "You should stick with skating, too," I said, being awkward.

"I will," he said, smiling and going with my bad joke.

"Maybe I'll take a video of my progress and show you sometime," I said.

"Sounds good," he said.

But he was just being nice. *Dang it.* I hated leaving him this way, but there was nothing else I could do. "Bye, Eric."

"Bye, Rose."

***

I felt sick to my stomach all evening and went to bed with an unsettled feeling.

I went through the motions of getting out of bed and getting dressed, but I was in a melancholy mood from the moment I woke up the following morning.

I went by Eric's room first thing, but he wasn't in there. His things were in there, but he was nowhere in sight. I checked outside on my way to the airport, but I couldn't find him. I felt heartbroken about leaving him. All morning, I had flashbacks of the summer we spent together. I wondered if he thought we were falling in love. I thought about what he could have heard me say on the phone. I knew I shouldn't make too much of it. I knew I was overthinking it. But I couldn't let it go.

***

I was still thinking about Eric when I got back to Chicago later that day. It was wrong of me to be torn up over one guy when I was dating another, so I called Charles that very evening and broke up with him over the phone.

Chapter 5

Five months later

It was already the first of December again. I had been at my new job for several months—long enough to know I didn't like it at all. It wasn't torturous, and I had a steady income with benefits, so I had no immediate plans to leave. But it wasn't what I dreamed about when I was on top of the world at my college newspaper. It was far from it.

Back then, social media was a part of my thing—a part of my life. But now I had to do so much of it for the jewelry company that I barely got on my personal accounts anymore. I was tied to my work phone, and my personal one often got neglected.

Today was Saturday, so both of them were neglected. I hadn't looked at either of my phones in hours. I was at my parents' house. I had come over for breakfast and to help my mom with some Christmas gift bags she always put together for my dad's coworkers at the TV studio. She wasn't normally the Susie-homemaker type, but these bags were a tradition. She and I were all set up at the dining room table, ready to start an assembly line.

I went to get my phone out of my purse so that I could put on some music for us. I walked into the kitchen, to the barstool where I had left my purse. I pulled out my phone and squinted at the name I saw flash across my screen.

I had a call from Eric Jones.

I started to call him right back, but I realized there was a voicemail, so I went to my voicemail instead. It was a call that came in an hour earlier. I pressed the button to play the message and held the phone to my ear.

My heart began pounding and excitement pulsed through my veins when I heard his voice.

"Hey, Rosie. How are you? I didn't mean to call. I have a customer who's right next to you in the… her name's Roseanne, and well… I was trying to call Ms. Roseanne, and I heard your voicemail. Your voice was sweet, and I didn't want to hang up, so… hello, Rose Cameron. I know you're not coming to Arkansas for Christmas. I hear Beau and Holland are looking forward to going up there and seeing you guys. Anyway, I hope all is well with you. Sorry for the long, random message. It's Eric Jones, by the way." *Beeeep!* I flinched at the sudden loud beeping sound.

I looked around, making sure that my mother was nowhere in sight before listening to the message again. Eric did not ask me to call him back, nor did he expect me to, but there was nothing I could do to stop myself. It was now or never. If I missed this opportunity, it would be awkward to call him later. I pressed the button before I could second-guess it.

His phone rang three times before he picked up.

I never once regretted calling, not even after he picked up. I was nervous and shaking, but I didn't regret it.

"Hello?" he answered.

"Hey," I said.

"Hey."

"You called me earlier," I said.

"Did you get my message?"

"Yeah, but I still called back because I haven't talked to you in so long. My brother is living in Arkansas, and even still, I know nothing about you—other than you left working at Uncle Max's and you're making docks full-time."

"Well, you know as much about me as I know about myself," he said.

"Was all that stuff right?" I asked. "You've got your own business?"

"I do. I don't have a storefront or anything. But I bought a truck and some tools, and I've got jobs lined up until April."

"Are you by yourself, or do you have guys working for you?"

"I do have guys. I pay them cash for now. I need to figure all that out. I have Landon's little brother, Zach, working with me. He's eighteen and not interested in college. And Billy—a guy I went to high school with. They both work with me full-time, but it's all happened so fast. I actually might need to look at hiring someone else to help me organize all this. I have to deal with enough crunching of numbers with bids and lumber costs. I need someone to help me with payroll." He laughed at himself. "Not that you needed to know any of that," he said.

"I wanted to know," I said. "I'm proud of you. I knew you could do it."

"I'm not quite doing it yet, but thank you. I'm headed in the right direction, at least."

"Did you say you got a truck?"

"Yeah, it's used, but it's like new, and I got a good deal on it. The guy only had it for six months."

"What color?"

"Grey. It's dark grey. I'm in the market for a trailer—a closed one. Right now, I have an open trailer, and it's not great in the rain, obviously. That's my next purchase."

"I'm proud of you, Eric."

"Thank you," he said, laughing a little. "What about you? How's your job going?"

"I'm good. It's good. Hang on." I put my hand over the phone so I didn't yell in Eric's ear. "I'm making a phone call!" I yelled since my mom had called for me.

She yelled, "Okay!" back like it was no big deal, and I put the phone to my ear again.

"Sorry," I said. "I'm over at my mom's."

"Oh."

"Why are you working on a Saturday?" I asked.

"How did you know I was working?"

"Because you tried to call Roseanne."

"That was just a phone call," he said with a smile in his voice. "But I am working. I'm wrapping up, actually. I was thinking of stopping at two. It's cold, and I've been working since eight."

"I ate lunch with my mom, and I'm about to help her put together gift bags for my dad's work."

"Okay, well, I'll let you go. Tell your mom 'hi' for me."

"I will. Do you think I can call you back?"

"Yeah, what do you mean?"

"I mean later, when I leave here. I was wondering if I could maybe call you back. I know it was an accident that we called, but I don't know. I haven't talked to you in a while, and I thought maybe we were getting cut off a little bit. You said you were leaving work, so I kind of thought that meant you wanted to talk."

"Yeah, I mean, if you think we're getting cut off, you can call me back."

He was being funny and saying it with a smile, and I stubbornly said, "Fine, I won't. Never mind."

"I'm just messing with you, Rose. But for real, I'm sure your boyfriend won't like it."

"What boyfriend?" I asked.

My heart started to pound when I said it because I realized he thought I still had a boyfriend. I wondered if that was why he was being aloof.

"That guy you're dating," he said.

"I'm not dating a guy," I assured him. "I broke up with Charles a long time ago."

"Oh, well, if there's no boyfriend, then yes, Rose, by all means, call me back." His voice. It was deep and familiar. I knew him well. I could picture that teasing, crooked half-smile.

"By all means?" I asked. "Who says that?"

"I do, in this case. Because I want you to *by all means* call me back. Why didn't you tell me you weren't dating that guy?"

"Would it have mattered?" I asked after a few seconds.

"Maybe," he said.

"Can I call you back in two hours?"

"Yes," he said.

***

"Hello?" Eric said as he picked up the phone two hours later.

"Hey, it's me, Rose."

"I know," he said.

"How are you?" I asked, nervously.

"I'm good. I'm fine. I stayed at the house and worked a little more, so I just left that job a minute ago. I still need a shower and everything."

"Do you want me to call you back?"

"No, I still have twenty minutes on the road. I'm in Broken Arrow, headed back toward Graham Springs."

"To your mom's?"

"No, it's my place," he said. "It's a one bedroom apartment. I rent it from a guy my dad knew from the hardware store. It's in his garage. I could probably get something a little bigger with the jobs I've been doing, but I don't want to overextend myself. I'm just getting used to saving money. I don't need a big place to live right now, anyway. Not till I'm ready to get married and have kids."

"Will you need a big place to live then?"

"Yes," he said. "That's the plan. That's the goal. If I keep working like I am, I think I can buy a nice house one day. I'll build it if I have to."

"Is that your goal? A house?"

"Yeah, probably. Why not? Real estate is always a good investment."

"No, I just… I'm happy for you. I didn't think I'd hear you say you were settling down. Are you going to stay in Arkansas? In Graham Springs?"

"For now. I don't know exactly where I'd build when I'm ready for that, but there's continual work here on the lake for a company that can build good patios and docks. I'm already good at it, and I'm getting better. My dad has taught me a lot. I'll start getting bigger jobs, and then from there, we'll get maintenance contracts. I'd love to eventually land a big contract at one of the marinas. That's what I'm shooting for."

"I'm proud of you."

"Thank you, but I'm the one who's impressed with you—making it in the big city. I guess you're still living by yourself. I know you moved out of your parents' place, and you said you broke up with that guy."

"I did say that," I said, smiling. "But I wasn't living with him, anyway."

"I know you weren't, and I know it probably bugs you that I did that."

"It doesn't bug me."

"Do you think I'm going to Hell for doing that?"

"What? No. What makes you say that?"

"I heard your Aunt Sarah giving AJ a hard time for that girl he brought over with him. She spent one night, and Sarah gave him a big lecture about keeping himself pure. I know your family is strict. They were really kind about letting me bring Jillian here for my sister's wedding and not saying anything to us. I didn't even think about it until I heard her correcting AJ. Anyway, I thought you might think I was destined for Hell with decisions like that."

"We all make bad decisions," I said. "We're all equally unworthy. And I know you're not going to Hell because we had a Jesus talk before. I mean, unless you changed your mind about that."

"No, I didn't change my mind. I was just... I thought you might think my living with someone was unforgivable."

"From a spiritual standpoint? No. Never. One sin is the same as the other. They all take us out of the running for perfection."

"What about from not a spiritual standpoint? Did I do the unforgivable from a personal standpoint? Does it discount me from finding love?"

"It depends on who you meet and marry. An action can be forgiven, but it still has consequences. I can't promise that it won't bug whoever you end up with."

"What about you? Does it bug you?"

My heart was beating like mad. It felt like it might rattle right out of my chest.

"Does what bug me?" I asked, stalling.

"Is it unforgivable for you, personally?"

"Are you asking if I would be able to date someone who had been in a long relationship previously?"

"Yes, I am asking that."

I paused for a second, catching my breath and deciding what I could possibly say to answer that. "I don't know," I said. "I've never been faced with that sort of choice."

"What if I asked you to go out on a date with me the next time you're in Arkansas? Would you go? Or would you reject me based on that fact?"

"How do you know that if I rejected you it would be because of that? I might just not like how you look."

"Ooh, ouch."

I laughed. "I'm joking. Who wouldn't love how you look? I obviously love how you look."

"You do?"

"Yes, Eric."

"What do you like about it?"

"Well, your eyes for one, but you know that already. You know what you look like. Don't make me reassure you when you know how handsome you are."

"But the Jillian thing is too much?" he asked. "No date?"

"Of course I would go on a date with you. You don't even have to ask that. We already spend a ton of time together every time I go there. If sitting across from each other and sharing a meal constitutes a date, we've already been on lots of dates."

"I'm not talking about the kind of dates we've already been on," he said. "Those were not dates. I'm talking about the kind where I kiss you at the end."

I laughed nervously because the feeling in my gut was overwhelming.

"What's so funny?"

"You. You're making me nervous talking like that."

"Good nervous?"

I was flaming hot with nerves and anticipation, and I was glad we were on the phone and Eric couldn't see me. "We'll have to see what's going on by the time I get back to Arkansas," I said. "Last Christmas you were with someone, and this summer, it was me. If you're dating someone again by the time I go to Arkansas again, you don't have to take me on a date. Or we could just hang out as friends like normal."

"Speaking of friends, how's the skating coming? How's the job? How are you? Tell me more about what you're doing."

"I only skate once a week, so I'm barely progressing at all. I need to go tonight, but I always put off going to the rink at night if I don't make any of the day classes. And even as these words come out of my mouth, I realize I'm full of excuses. I'm going tonight. I'll just work on skating and have fun—not put any pressure on myself."

"Do you go by yourself, or with someone?"

"I have a few people I can text—a couple of people I met from the rink, and also my friend, Caroline, from work. She skates."

"You're going to have to tell me about work," he said. He sighed. "I've got this guy calling me on the other line about a job."

"Go take it," I said.

"Can I call you later? I want to hear how your work is going. Oh, wait, I forgot, you're going skating."

"No, no, it's not till later tonight. You can call me back."

"Okay, I will," he said with a smile in his voice.

I hung up the phone in the best mood. I was beyond excited to be in touch with Eric again.

Chapter 6

I did not end up going skating that night.

Eric called me, and we stayed on the phone for the next eight hours. I went through the motions of getting things done in my apartment. I ate and changed clothes and cleaned and was somewhat productive as a human, but it was all absentminded because we stayed on the phone for an incredibly long time.

This same thing happened for the next month. It wasn't quite eight hours a day, but we talked a lot—at least two hours a day. We didn't feel obligated to make it happen, but we wanted to.

Talking every day for weeks made Eric feel like my new best friend. I had never had so much fun talking to someone. In our adult life, there had not been a time when we were around each other when one of us wasn't seeing someone else.

We liked each other's company, obviously, but spending time getting to know each other on the phone was different. We didn't feel like we had to define what was going on.

It had been a month now. The first of the year had come and gone, and almost every single day, I talked to Eric. There was no pressure to do it. We both seemed like we wanted to make it happen.

Eric focused a lot of attention on his business, so I was in on some of the decisions he made. I had been exposed to certain aspects of business at the newspaper and now at the jewelry company. I was happy to offer any advice or help I could. His sister and my cousin owned a successful construction company in Florida, and they gave him advice, too.

Eric was working hard, and also making a lot of effort when he was off the job. I respected him for that, and it was inspiring to hear about how much his customers loved his work and that it was resulting in more jobs being booked.

About half of our time on the phone was spent by me helping him with his work. I liked it that way. It was fun for me, and I knew that he was at a place in his life where he wanted to go all in on a goal. I had a natural desire to cheer him along and help him in any way I could.

He helped me, too. He held me accountable with my skating, encouraging me to stick with it a few times a week so that I would see improvements. I didn't have any problem making time to skate once I knew Eric had an interest in my progress. I wanted to get better by the next time I saw him. We already established that would take place the following summer.

We talked about life, and we got to know each other well, but never did we put a label on our relationship. There was no need to when we lived in different states and there was no chance of us seeing each other.

Then came the moment when all that changed.

We were talking on the phone one night in January when the conversation started.

"Your birthday's next week," I said.

"Yes, it is."

"I got you something."

"What is it?" he asked.

"I'm going to mail it to you. Are you ever going to tell me where you and Landon are going to spend the night?"

"No."

"Why not?"

"You wouldn't approve."

"And you said it happens on the weekend?"

"It doesn't have to, but yes. We're doing it on the weekend since we all work during the week."

"Is it breaking and entering?"

"N-no. It's not that. Not exactly."

"Why can't you tell me?"

"Because. Well, now that you think it's worse than it is… it's just a cave."

"A cave? Why would I disapprove?"

"I don't know, it's not exactly our cave. I mean, it's not exactly trespassing, it's just a tiny, little bit of it. It's no big deal. We've done it for eight out of the last ten years."

"What is it? A cave on someone's private property."

"Yeah, it's about three hours from here—at Cosmic Cavern. It's a whole big tourist place that's open to the public. But Landon's family has a farm over there, connected to it. There's some of his family's land that goes into a back entrance. It's nowhere near the public entrance, and it's way back in the woods. It's blocked off now, but it used to be a hole in the ground. Landon's great-great-granddad found it when he was a kid. There's a ladder now, but it's primitive, and you have to climb down into a dark cave and then through a tight passageway, but then it opens up to one of the big caverns. It's one that tourists go through, but we enter through a hidden passage on the far side. It's gorgeous. And it's no colder in there in the winter than it is in the summer. It's always sixty-five degrees. It's freaky, though, if you've never been in a cave. They have lights on during tourist season, but right now, it's just whatever lights we take."

"You're going to a sleepover in a dark cave?"

"Yes. It sounds sketchy when you say it like that but it's fun. Landon's been in there fifty times. He did it all the time when he was a kid. I feel like they know we do it, otherwise, they would've made his family block off that entrance. That's his family's hole, fair and square. His great-great-grandfather fell into it and almost killed himself when he was a kid. It's safe now. Safer, at least. There's a ladder, and it's been dug out in spots where it was really tight. We take sleeping bags and flashlights, and we set up a little camp. The main cave people don't know. They're closed from New Year's through February. That's why we always do it for my birthday."

"Your birthday is Thursday and you're camping Saturday?"

"Yep."

"You are crazy."

"I know. I'm sorry. I thought you might not approve. I just figured I should tell you in light of you thinking it was worse than it was."

"It is better than I thought."

"Good," he said.

"Not that it matters what I think."

"Yes, it does," he said.

"You mean if I said don't do it, you wouldn't go?"

"I know you well enough to know you wouldn't say that. It's a birthday tradition. Landon said we're doing it every year till one of us has a kid."

"That's the rule?"

"Yeah, that's what he said. That's when we have to settle down."

"I kind of want to go with you."

"You do?" he asked, sounding completely shocked.

"Would I be able to? I've never done anything like that—not even close. Could we get arrested?"

"I mean, there's a slight chance, but I don't think so. I sleep like a baby every time I'm down there, so that tells you how worried I am."

"Will you take me back over there when I get some vacation time this summer?"

"I would, but it's a cool sixty-five all year around. You might as well take a sick day and come with us for my birthday."

"Next we—" I had to clear my throat because my voice gave out. "Next weekend?" I asked.

"Yeah, but I know you said you can't make it down here until summer. I thought I'd try my luck."

"I wish I could," I said. "I could maybe take a sick day or two." My heart felt like it might jump out of my chest when I said those words.

It was at that moment that feelings hit me.

I was confronted with possibly seeing Eric in the near future, and the excitement I felt about it was electric. There was no question that I would take off work and go down there to see him for his birthday.

"I would freak out if you could come over here this weekend."

"Would Landon let a third person go along?"

"Yes. There's usually like four or five of us. Avery has these inflatable mats. They're so comfortable. She'll bring as many as we need."

"Oh, it's a whole party? I didn't know that."

"Not a whole party—just three or four of us. And it's really laid back. Avery's my second cousin. She's been coming with us for years. It might only be us three. It doesn't matter. I want you to come no matter how many of us there are. Please come. Are you seriously even thinking about it?"

I could hear the excitement in his voice, and it caused a hot, electric feeling to happen in my body. Oh, my goodness. This was too much. I was short of breath at the thought of coming face-to-face with Eric.

"Y-yes, I'm, I'm actually thinking about it. I don't know how much flights cost. I Googled that place you were talking about just now, and it's a nine-hour drive. I have to fly. That's going to mean landing in Little Rock. I could maybe try to leave work early on Friday and then call in on Monday. That would put me back to work Tuesday."

"Yes. Please."

His voice. It caused an ache in my belly to hear him plead with me to come. We had been talking for a month, and now suddenly my feelings were out of control.

"I have to check on flights."

"I'll help you. I mean, no pressure, but if it comes down to money, I will help you with a ticket. I think it would make my birthday an A-plus, one hundred kind of day if you come over here and go in that cave with me."

"A-plus, one hundred? I'm really going to try to do that. Let me search some flights, and I'll call you back."

"Really?"

"Yes, really," I said, smiling. "I'm going to call you back."

Chapter 7

I did not care how much money it cost. I did not care if I lost my job over it. I was going to Arkansas for Eric's birthday and going down in that cave, come rain or come shine.

I hung up with him and I purchased the most expensive airline ticket I had ever bought. My parents normally were the ones asking me to make a trip to Arkansas, and they always paid for my travel there. I wasn't sure how much they normally paid for a round-trip ticket, but I was relatively sure it wasn't twenty-six hundred dollars. I was thankful I even had a credit card with that high of a limit.

***

Five days later, I touched down in Little Rock, Arkansas.

"Hey sister, how are you?"

I hugged my brother, Beau, when he picked me up from the airport. I had seen him recently when he came to Chicago for Christmas, but I gave him a tight hug. He was a man. He had gotten married and was now living with his wife at my Uncle Max's house where he was working with Max doing a building design and construction on the property. It was fairly top secret, so my brother didn't talk about it. We all knew to be cool and not ask questions about Uncle Max's job.

I saw him as some kind of mafia Godfather—only instead of suits and ties, he had a Florida, island style. The theory of he and Casey being modern-day pirates had also been thrown out there. Max had three sons. Casey was part of whatever mafia-pirate-adventure-seeking club Max was in. Caleb and Charlie were more straight-laced. I knew my brother was currently living at the lake house, but I hadn't even bothered asking who else was out there.

I talked to my brother about it on our way back to the house from the airport. I learned that Casey and Max were both at the lake house with Beau, Holland, and Paul who lived there. Five people was nothing on that property. With only five other people there besides Eric and me, I knew it would feel empty and quiet. January was one of the times of the year when everyone was living in their respective cities and doing their own thing. Charlie and Hope spent a lot of time in Arkansas since that was her home state, and even they weren't there. Those two were currently back in Miami.

My brother, Beau, did not know about the sleepover I had planned for Saturday night. For whatever reason, I hadn't shared that bit of information with him. I knew he assumed I would be staying at the house all three nights of my trip, and I hadn't yet sensed an appropriate time to bring it up.

"Eric called me a little while ago and asked if I could come get you," he said.

"I know. I was expecting Eric."

"He had a thing with his mom," Beau explained. "She got bit by a snake."

"I heard. He texted me. What happened? Did he talk to you about it?"

My brother shrugged. "He went with her to the hospital. They gave her anti-venom, but her leg was swollen. I don't think it was that bad. He's coming back to the house tonight."

"That's what his text said, but I didn't have details about the snake bite."

"Yeah, I guess she moved some big potted plant and disturbed it."

"Is that something that happens here?" I asked since I didn't even think about it with the camping trip.

"No, it's rare. I never hear about it. His mom was a fluke. I guess it had a nest under a big barrel planter, and she moved it and disturbed it. Are you and Eric a thing?"

"No. I mean, we talk a lot, and I'm pretty much here for his birthday, but no. We're just friends. At least right now."

"What's that mean, at least right now?"

"I don't know, Beau. I like him, but I live in Chicago and he lives in Arkansas. And we're not like that. We don't act like we like each other. We're just friends."

"He said he was taking you camping Saturday night. Is that true?"

"That is true, but it's with a group of people. It's not just us two."

Beau was quiet for a long time as he drove.

It was so long that eventually, I said, "What are you thinking?"

"I don't know. I like Eric. But I can't see him wanting to live in Chicago. He likes to be outside too much, and Chicago's freezing five months out of the year."

"No one's moving anywhere," I said.

"Okay," he said, disbelieving.

"I won't lie, though, Beau. I'm excited to see him. I have to play it cool because we're not like that with each other, but I'm nervous. I like him so much."

"I should've seen this coming. You know you missed his birthday. It was yesterday."

"I know, but it's this camping trip I'm trying to go on. He mentioned it, and I've never been camping."

"Where is it?"

"It's at Landon's great-grandpa's farm. Three hours away."

"It's too cold to go camping."

"I think it's a cabin or something—it's some place Landon knows about. It's not cold."

"You're not usually a camping type."

"I know."

"But you like Eric?"

"Yes. Do you not like him?"

"No, I love Eric. I just didn't know you liked him until right now. I didn't even know you were coming until a few days ago."

"It was all really last minute."

"Eric had a bunch of people over at the house yesterday for his birthday."

"I know. Uncle Max told him to invite some friends."

We rode for another minute in silence as I wondered what Beau had seen from his point of view.

"Do you like his friends?" I asked.

"I do," he said thoughtfully. "Uncle Max wouldn't let Eric have people over if he didn't like him. He said he misses having Eric around since he got his own place and doesn't work at the house anymore. Uncle Max said he's going to build him a skateboard ramp just to get him back over there. We never see him anymore."

"I don't know what to think about Eric," I said. "I like him, but he doesn't know that. We said something about going on a date, and we flirt, but then the moment passes. It would really embarrass me if you mention it, though, Beau. We're just friends, and I don't want either of us to be on the spot about it during this trip. Just let me play it off like we're friends."

"I can't believe you like Eric Jones."

"Why not?"

"I don't know. He's completely opposite from that last guy you dated, for one, and two... I don't know. I just never thought. Holland said she saw something with him and you this summer, but I didn't. I thought you wanted that guy with the fancy job."

"I don't care about jobs."

"Well, I happen to like Eric, so it's hard for me to advise you against him."

"Then don't," I said.

Beau glanced at me from across the console. He opened his mouth to say something but then changed his mind. When I finally spoke again, it was to ask about his wife and their dog collar business. They also had a dog named Ralphie, and we spent the rest of the time talking about him and Holland. I was glad to have the subject change because I didn't know what to feel about Eric. We talked about Beau's life until we got back to the house.

It was dinner time when Beau and I made it to Broken Arrow, and Holland had food prepared when we got there. She had cooked, and the house smelled delicious when we came in. It was chicken chili, and the three of us, along with Uncle Max, all sat around, eating dinner and catching up.

It was a couple of hours later when Eric arrived. He had texted from the hospital in Little Rock, so I knew when he was on his way, but there was nothing that could have prepared me for seeing him.

Eric was looking better than ever. His hair had gotten longer and was hanging over his forehead, and he pushed it back with a gloriously casual motion. He was dressed in layers—jeans with a shirt and a light jacket. He came in while we were all sitting around the living room, and I stood up and made my way over to him to greet him and give him a hug.

I went in for the embrace even though my brother and Holland were right there in the room with us. Eric hugged me back, gripping onto me just enough that my heart stopped. He was here. He was here, and I was here. My brain could not function properly for a moment. I got stuck in my own thoughts as I struggled to resolve this being the same man I talked to every day. Seeing Eric in person reminded me of how strikingly handsome he was, and that brought back all those feelings I had before.

This was the first time our paths crossed at a time when we could actually be attracted to each other, and that knowledge made me breathless. *Could he possibly be the same person I had been talking to every day? Could this be the man I laughed and talked with all the time?*

"How's your mom?" I asked after we hugged and I stepped back. The others seemed to be giving us a little space.

"She's fine. I'm sorry that took so long. I had to wait for her to get discharged so I could give her a ride back. She's dating a guy, but he was working, so I needed to be there. I'm sorry."

"I'm just glad she's okay. That kind of freaks me out a little bit, thinking about Saturday night." I spoke quietly enough that no one could overhear me.

"There are no snakes in that cave," he assured me, confidently. "And they're dormant this time of year, anyway. Nothing like this ever happens. I promise you won't get hurt. My mom was out in the woods."

He whispered all of that to me before Uncle Max walked over to us. He gave Eric a handshake and a half-hug.

"Beau and Holland are staying up, but I think I'm heading to the back," Uncle Max said. "I have some things to take care of before I turn in for the night. Welcome, Rose, glad you're here, baby."

"Thank you, Uncle Max."

"Eric, I know you have your own place, but you know that bedroom's always yours if you don't feel like getting back on the road tonight."

"Thank you," Eric said. "I might take you up on that."

I watched as Uncle Max hugged Eric, and then I hugged him when he turned to me. "Night," I said to him.

He grinned and pointed at us. "Night. Don't stay up too late, you two." There was a wry smile involved when he said it, and the nervous feeling in my gut intensified.

Chapter 8

Eric Jones

Eric and Rose stayed up, talking to Beau and Holland. They found a deck of cards and played spades because Eric, Beau, and Rose had all played it as children. They had to teach Holland, but she was a quick learner, and they had fun and were competitive, as always.

Eric could not keep his eyes off of Rose Cameron. He could not stop looking at her or thinking about her. She was there with him, and he was awestruck. She got on a plane and came to Arkansas. She sat across from him at the table, and they never made any physical contact, but her presence in the room was enough. Eric was wound up tight like a spring.

He had liked Rose Cameron since they were kids, but she was older than him and had never been interested. By the time their paths crossed as adults, he was dating someone else.

Eric had always been an impulsive guy. He was quick to make decisions and run with them. At the time, years earlier, it didn't register that there might be consequences for getting an apartment with Jillian Meyers. He had a girlfriend, and rent was a lot cheaper when they both paid it, so they moved in together. Period. That was the extent of the thought he had put into it. He had no idea Rose would come back into his life.

Eric had spent a lot of time with Rose this summer. She was the one who had a boyfriend this time, but oddly enough, Eric felt that wasn't the problem. He thought he could beat out this other guy when it came to making Rose happy, but the problem was that she had lost some feelings for him during the Jillian thing. He wasn't sure what she had lost, if it was respect or something else, but it had happened as a result of him being with another woman. Rose was dating someone that summer, but that other man wasn't the only thing standing in his way with her. She was closed off to him in ways that he knew were deeper than the fact that she had a boyfriend.

Even during the last month, while they were talking on the phone, she was closed off. He knew she wasn't dating anyone else, and he still didn't feel like he had a chance with her. He honestly couldn't believe it when she said she wanted to come to Arkansas for his birthday. He thought he was dreaming when she said she bought a ticket, and now there she was, in the same room, playing cards and laughing and staring at him with a smile from across the table.

"We need to turn in," Holland said. "It's after eleven."

"Where are you going tomorrow?" Beau asked.

"Berryville. It's Landon's family's farm," Eric said. Beau nodded, looking Eric over. It was one of those man-to-man glances where Beau was trying to gauge Eric's intentions.

"I'll keep her out of trouble," Eric said, standing up with Beau and Holland as they got up. "We make this camping trip every year," he added.

Beau nodded.

"We're not leaving till noon or one, so I'll see you in the morning," Rose said.

Holland and Beau hugged her and said goodnight before making their way to the guest house where they were staying. Rose glanced at Eric, and his chest felt tight. He had to have her. It took all of his strength to remain calm and not take her into his arms right then. He cleared his throat to speak, but she was already about to say something.

"Do you want to go down to the lake?" she asked.

"Yes, I do." Eric didn't care where Rose wanted to go, the answer was 'yes'. "It's cold, so you better bundle up."

She looked at him. "You promise we'll be okay tomorrow? We won't be too cold or get snake-bit?"

He grinned at her. She was adorable. "No, we're not going to get too cold or snake-bit," he assured her. "I promise I wouldn't put you in danger. It's a tiny bit of danger, but not real danger," he added.

They put on coats and went to the lake to sit on the dock. There was a small house down there, and they went inside some of the time and stayed outside some, letting the cold wind hit them. They had a normal conversation with each other. It was just like they picked up where they left off all the times they spoke on the phone. They didn't talk about being attracted to each other, or having any kind of relationship. And every second that went by, Eric had to fight against the urge to bring it up—to kiss her.

It was after midnight when they went back into the house and made their way down the hall. Eric's bedroom was all the way across the house from the one where Rose was staying, but he walked toward hers.

"I'm staying the night here," he said.

"I figured. It's late."

"I have to run to my apartment in the morning. I'm going to get up early and drive over there. I need to pack some things and take care of a few emails before we take off."

Rose nodded. "I'll see you when you get back."

"I'll come back here by eleven thirty, enough time to help you get everything packed."

"What time are the others getting here?"

"Avery's always running late," he said. "But I told her I want to get on the road no later than one o'clock. I said we're leaving with or without her."

Rose hesitated by her bedroom door, standing in the threshold with it half open.

"Goodnight, Rose," he said, looking at her, aching to hold her. "I'm happy you're here. Thank you for being here."

"Goodnight, to you, too, Eric. I'm happy, too. I'm even happier than you, I bet."

He smirked, side-eyeing her. "I don't think so," he said, shaking his head confidently. "If there's a contest about who's happier right now at this moment, I win. I'm in Heaven with you here, Rose. I have my own apartment with my own bed, and I'm not even sleeping in it because I want to be near you."

She stared down shyly before taking a step into her room. She bit her lip and took a deep breath inward, looking like she was too nervous to do anything but say goodnight.

"Goodnight," she said breathlessly.

"Goodnight," he said.

She smiled at him as she closed the door.

What in the world?

Why did they let that happen?

Eric stood there for a second, letting everything sink in before turning to make his way to the other side of the house.

His phone was in his back pocket, and he checked it because he could feel that several notifications had gone off since the last time he had looked at it. There were a couple of phone calls from Landon, so Eric called him back.

"Where are you?" was how Landon answered the phone. "I went by your house at eleven o'clock and you weren't there."

"I'm at Max's house."

"Are you sleeping over there?"

"Yes, why?"

"I need to borrow a water bottle. Mine got lost. Do you have an extra one I can take on the trip?"

"Yes, and I'll be at home by eight in the morning if you want to come by before we come here. Otherwise, I'll just have it with me when I meet you here."

"Are you with Rose?"

"Right now? No."

"But she's there?"

"Yes, she's here. I've been with her all night— after that ordeal with my mom."

"What happened with your mom?"

"I'll tell you about it tomorrow."

"I meant are you *with* her? Are y'all together? Did you kiss her?"

"Landon."

"What?"

"It's none of your business if I kissed a woman."

"That means you did."

"No, I didn't. I actually didn't."

"Why not?"

"I don't know. She closed the door."

"I thought she was into you. I thought that's why she came on this whole trip."

"Do not say that when you see her tomorrow," Eric said.

"I know how to be cool," Landon said.

"Okay, I'm going to let you go. I'll talk to you in the morning."

"Oh, okay," Landon said. "I'll talk to you in the morning."

Eric hung up his phone and slid it into the pocket of his jeans. He took a step into the spare bedroom where he would be sleeping, but he stopped in his tracks. The first question Landon asked was whether or not he had kissed Rose. It was even on Landon's mind. Eric wanted to do it. *Had she wanted it to happen?* There were several moments during the night when he felt like he was on the verge of trying and had to stop himself. In those moments, he didn't feel like she wanted it to happen.

But he wanted it badly enough, and he was curious enough that he turned and headed back through the house, toward her bedroom. He had no plan. He had no idea what he would do or say once he got to her door.

He was not expecting to find it open, but it was.

Rose's door, the same door that was closed moments ago was now open about a foot.

"Hello?" he called, leaning toward it cautiously.

Within seconds, she rushed to the door, standing in the doorway, taking up the whole crack with her body. Eric could not help but smile at the way she suddenly appeared way in the opening. She was the cutest thing he had ever seen.

"What are you doing?" she asked.

"I came back here to see if... why is your door open?"

"What did you come to see?"

"You."

"That's why my door is open."

"What do you mean?" he asked.

"Well, if you were to come back here, and it was closed, then what's to stop you from turning around and going back to your side of the house?"

"Yeah, what's to stop me?" he said, staring at her. He was lost in her eyes, lost in her face. He wanted to take her into his arms and hold her so tightly that he could absorb her into himself.

"Do you like me, Eric?"

His gut ached when she said those words. *Did he like her? Of course he liked her.* He was taken aback by the obvious question.

"Yes," he said.

She held onto the door frame shyly. "I know you like me as a friend, but I'm talking about more than a friend."

"I'm definitely talking about more than a friend."

"Well then, why didn't you ever ki—"

He was already moving towards her by the time she started the sentence, and his mouth touched hers right when she started to say the word.

Her lips were like honey-covered heaven.

Eric was broken, aching with need and desire for her. Rose was so precious to him. It took everything in his power to use restraint, to touch her gently. He let his lips rest against hers for several seconds. Their mouths softened, and she stayed there, holding the contact and not pulling away. They finally broke apart, and he pulled back only to kiss her a second and then a third time. Each time, he let his mouth linger on hers. On the third one, he reached up and touched her cheek. Her skin and her lips were like velvet—she was like an actual Rose, and his heart felt like it might explode. He had never in his life exercised such restraint as he did right then.

He straightened, pulling back and staring at her. "Thank you," he said. "Thank you for leaving your door open."

"Did you get what you came over here for?" she asked.

"Yes," he said. "So, thank you, and goodnight. That's a much better way to say goodnight." He gave her a slight, sideways grin as he stepped back.

"I agree," she said. "That was better. And thank you for walking back over here. I was hoping this would happen."

She smiled shyly at him and Eric felt like he couldn't take it. He wanted to kidnap her and run away to Las Vegas to get married. He felt so much pent-up love and energy that he could just about do something crazy like that. Instead, he told her goodnight and went to bed.

Chapter 9

Rose Cameron

I had a difficult time going to sleep that night. Eric's lips had been on mine, and I replayed the moment in my head more times than I probably should have. His lips had been on mine. After all these years, Eric's lips finally touched mine. It was so distracting that my body could not find sleep until the middle of the night.

I had my alarm set for 8am, but I didn't need it. I was still so mentally pumped that I woke up before it went off. I looked at the clock at seven thirty, and in spite of only getting a few hours of sleep, I felt wide awake. I knew that Eric would be leaving, so I texted him the second my eyes opened.

Me:
Are you still here at the house?

I heard back from him within a minute. It was a call. I answered, trying to sound fully awake even though I clearly was not.

"Hello," I said.

"Hey, I'm driving, so I couldn't text."

"Oh, okay, you're already on the road?"

"Yeah, I left about fifteen minutes ago. I can come back, though. Do you need me?"

"No, no. I woke up and thought I might catch you before you left."

"Did you need something?"

"No, I just wanted to tell you good morning."

"Oh. Really? Good morning. I thought you might sleep in."

"I tried to. My eyes just opened. I texted you about three seconds after that, so I'm still sleepy."

"I'm tired, too, but I know what you mean. I woke up before my alarm. I'm headed to my apartment."

"Okay," I said. "I'll see you when you get back."

***

It was eleven when Eric arrived, and by that time, I was all packed and ready to go. There were only four of us going—Landon, Avery, Eric, and myself. Eric's truck fit the four of us comfortably and was the nicest vehicle we had access to, so we drove that. Avery got motion sickness when she sat in the back, so I sat in the back with Landon. It wasn't a big deal. I never had a problem with riding in the backseat, and I wasn't going to protest just so that I could sit next to Eric (although I did want to sit next to him).

The trip took over three hours, but we all talked the whole time, and it went by quickly.

Landon's great-grandparents were home in the farmhouse, but he was the only one who went inside.

Avery and I got out of the truck, but Eric stayed inside because he had to tend to something on his phone. Zack and Billy were on a job today, and they had a question for him. Landon had gone into the house using the back door, and us girls hung out on a stretch of driveway that was between the truck and the door.

"Sorry," Eric said, when he finished on his phone and walked over there to meet us.

Just then, Landon came out of the house, and he was carrying a plate of cookies and smiling at us as he chewed one of them.

"You guys can come inside. My great-grandparents aren't in here," he said with his mouth full. He held out the plate and we all came toward him to take a cookie.

"My Grams left a note saying we can use the den and downstairs bathroom without bugging them."

"These are good," Eric said.

"They are good," I agreed. They were oatmeal raisin with chocolate chips. They were hearty and old-fashioned, and I felt right at home at that old farmhouse. I had been to similar homes as a young child. I couldn't recall an exact time or place, but the small, older home felt comfortable and familiar.

We went inside and hung out for a while before heading off to our adventure. The sun was setting as Eric drove us to the woods at the back of the property. It was about a half-mile. Then we got out and hiked a few hundred yards to the entrance to the cave. The sun was fading fast, and it was even darker in the woods.

The entrance of the cave didn't look like much. There was a shack in the middle of the woods with a small fence around it. There were signs posted about trespassing, but everything was overgrown and no one in their right mind would want to go in there, anyway.

Landon had a key to the padlock on the gate. It took him a minute to get it open, but he finally did.

It was late in the afternoon and it was January, so it was getting darker by the minute.

"This is easily the craziest thing I've ever done," I said as he worked. I was unable to stand still, and I shifted my weight from foot to foot. I had dressed for the cold weather, so my shaking wasn't from the temperature.

They all smiled calmly at me when I glanced around.

"The first few times we did it, I was scared out of my mind," Avery said. "With those lakes in there, I seriously thought some prehistoric lake monster was going to come up and swallow me whole. I made Landon and Eric build a wall around me. Henry was coming with us back then, too."

"Lake monsters, I hadn't thought of that. Thanks, Avery," I said in a sarcastic tone, causing them all to laugh.

There were two underground lakes in this cavern. I had done some research and knew a little of what it looked like from inside. I could not, however, believe that I was going inside it through a forbidden back entrance. This way in was contained inside of a literal shack. I knew the path down would be narrow and steep, and I could not imagine what kind of hole I was about to climb into.

Landon unlocked the door and shined a light inside before turning to us, shaking his head with an eye-rolling smile. "Eighty-two years old, and still doing this *danger-keep-out* stuff."

I peered inside, and saw a handwritten sign on notebook paper that read, *"Danger, Posted, Warning, Do Not Go Inside,"* but then, Landon aimed the flashlight just below the sign, and there were two plastic zipper bags—both full of food. One was full of sandwiches and the other had more cookies. There was another note on those that said, "Have fun, Love, Grams and Gramps Hansen."

"She cut the crust off of the sandwiches," I said.

"She always does," Avery said.

Landon placed the bags into his backpack before opening a small wooden door and shining the light down the hole.

"Okay, this first part is steep enough that we're going down on a ladder, but I'll get down to the landing first and have a light on down there so y'all can see. There are steps after that."

Landon was looking at me and talking to me since everyone else had done it before and knew what was going on.

"I'll help her," Eric said. He reached out and touched the side of my arm when he said it, and I took a step closer to him. This caused him to hold onto me.

I glanced at him when he did that. Our eyes met, and we stayed locked in eye contact while Landon turned and began to climb down the passageway. I needed Eric. I wasn't thinking about chickening out, but I was reluctant about climbing into a hole in the earth. I could not believe I was in a shack and about to climb into an actual cave and spend the night in it. The whole underground lake was too much for me to comprehend. I glanced behind me.

"There used to be a rock covering this," Avery said, seeing me look around. "And the way down used to be way sketchier than it is now."

"Yeah, but that was before our time," Eric added. He held onto the sleeve of my coat. "It's always been easy like this since we've been coming here."

"Hope was always so terrified," Avery said. "She hates the darkness. She's only come twice, and both times, she went back and slept at the farmhouse."

"That's an option?" I asked, glancing at Eric.

"Are you afraid?" he asked.

I shook my head, assuring him.

Landon was already up to his chest in the hole, going down the ladder. He had a headlamp on, and I could see in my periphery as Avery strapped hers to her head. We all had several flashlights and lanterns in our possession. Avery had an extra bag which she lowered on a pre-existing rope when Landon got to the bottom and yelled up for her. Eric went to help her, and I watched the whole thing, standing back so I didn't get in the way. They also lowered Avery's backpack and mine so that we wouldn't have to tote them down the ladder.

Eric stepped back while Avery got situated to climb down the ladder. I went toward him, and he looked at me, reaching out for me as I came near him.

"Are you okay? Are you scared?" He took me into his arms, and I went readily.

"I'm a little scared, but I'm excited. I'm happy to know that chickening out is an option if I freak out."

Eric held onto me but he pulled back just far enough to look down at me, his ice-blue eyes were still shining even in the darkness. "We can leave absolutely anytime. My truck's right there. You just say the word, and I will drive you back to Broken Arrow—back to Chicago if you need it."

"Thank you," I said.

I felt intimidated at the moment, and my voice reflected that. Eric wrapped his arms all the way around me as we waited for Avery to descend the ladder. He was not shy with his grasp. He stood behind me and completely enveloped me in his embrace, holding me tightly.

"Thank you for being here," he said, speaking softly near my ear.

I could smell the warm, dank smell of the cave, and that combined with the sound of his voice in my ear made me weak in the knees. I leaned into him, reaching back and holding onto him with a handful of his jacket. I could smell Eric along with the cave, and it was the scent of a wonderful, exhilarating adventure.

"I'm excited about it," I said, looking down into the hole after Avery climbed down, and knowing that utter darkness was down there. "Scared and excited at the same time," I added. I put my headlamp on, and Eric did the same.

From that point forward, Eric kept a protective hand on me. He went down ahead of me, and he called me down, helping me situate myself on the ladder, and staying a few rungs below me with a hand on my legs.

Once we reached the landing, we got our bags and headed down the path. Everything was damp. It was slippery and was sometimes steep, so in parts of it we stooped down to keep our balance. Eric walked in front of me, looking back constantly and telling me where to step and what to expect, drawing me forward.

It was about a fifteen-minute hike since we were walking slowly and watching our step. We had to traverse a few narrow passageways on our way to the larger cavern where we would set up camp. Eric only let go of me a few times, and it was in places where it was so tight that it wasn't physically possible to hold my hand.

It was significantly warmer in the cave than it was outside, and we all shed our jackets when we got to the landing place where we would spend the night.

Chapter 10

I could only see a foot or two in front of my face, but it was enough to know that I was completely unfamiliar with my utterly black surroundings. The headlamps provided enough light that I had already seen some stalactites and stalagmites. Everything was tan and wet and shiny, and I felt like I had got into a spaceship and landed on another planet. I was sort of thankful that I couldn't see beyond a few feet.

They knew just what area to go to once we found the open room, and we set down our bags and began to unpack. Within a minute, there were a few high-powered lanterns set around our small area. Even then, we could hardly see a thing. It was as if there was a dome of light around us and then complete blackness on the other side of it. I had never experienced anything like it, and I moved slowly, letting myself take it all in.

It took the better part of an hour to completely set up. Avery had inflatable pads that were similar to those mats you lay on in a swimming pool. They were made for camping and surprisingly comfortable. We set them up with blankets, and then we finally sat down and got situated, all gathered around in the small dome of light created by our lanterns. They had a high-powered flashlight, and they aimed it around, showing me the various cave formations.

I gazed around at their faces after they turned that light off and we were back to the lantern lights. They all smiled at me. They looked comfortable, like this was a normal thing to do with your Saturday night.

"This is by far the wildest thing I have ever done," I said, speaking quietly. "I know you guys got together the other day, but I missed Eric's birthday, so," I hesitated and glanced at Eric. "I got you something. Do you want to open it?"

"You got me something?"

"Yeah, and it's… you don't have to use it, because it's a matter of taste, and I don't know if you'll like it, but yeah, I did get you something. It's just for fun. You don't have to do anything with it." I went silent after that short rant, and Eric just stared at me, trying to make sense of what I had said. "Let me get it. I think you'll see what I'm saying once you open it."

I was big on presentation. I had learned that from my mother who was an expert at inspecting things and making sure they followed strict guidelines. She had taught me the importance of packaging and presentation, and I had put a lot of work into Eric's gift. It was something I had been working on before I ever had plans to come to Arkansas for his birthday.

"Originally, I was going to mail this, but I figured since I decided to come, I'd just hang onto it."

I said that to explain the fact that his address was written on the outside of the box. I didn't have it taped, and Eric easily peeled back the flaps and looked inside. He took the smaller box out and opened it. We all watched patiently. Avery began humming the birthday song slowly and I joined in with her, mumble-singing the lyrics as we watched Eric open the gift.

It was a leather portfolio, and he took it out of its box, marveling at the construction of it and the fact that it had his initials, ERJ, engraved on the outside.

"Look inside," I said.

He opened it, wearing a curious expression.

There were only four of us sitting around, so Eric and I weren't touching or making contact in any way. There were a few feet of space between us all. Eric opened it, glanced down at it, and then leaned to the side, rolling onto his arm and collapsing with his head landing on my leg for a second before he sat up. I reached out and touched him, touching the back of his hair and the warm skin on his neck while he was in front of me. He stared at me after he came up.

"This is unbelievable," he said. He glanced at Avery and then at Landon. "She had that logo you drew made into a whole brand with my name and everything." He opened the portfolio again and stared down into it. "It says E. Jones Patio and Dock.

She made letterhead and business cards. It's a whole set." He looked up at me. "Is this mine?"

I nodded. "Landon had come up with a cool design," I said. "I just had it styled up with your name and everything. I wasn't sure if you would like the font, but I did the best I could. I worked with a guy in our design room. I wanted it to be a surprise."

"It's unbelievable. I love it. I'm blown away." He passed the portfolio to Landon who began checking it out. Avery went over to Landon and started looking over his shoulder.

"I don't know what to say," Eric said, turning to me.

The cave was so dark that I could feel the smothering darkness, and I didn't care. As long as I saw his face, I was fine. Eric was comforting to me from so long ago that I trusted him with my life. I knew he was the type of person who would do anything for me. He would drop his life and run to Chicago if I ever needed him to.

"Do you like it?" I asked.

"It's amazing," Landon said.

"I love this so much," Avery added. I could see them from the corner of my eyes, and she pointed her flashlight directly at the portfolio.

"I'm taking it to my truck," Eric said suddenly. "And Rose is coming with me. We'll be back in thirty minutes."

"Hey, can you go up to the house while you're on land and get some hot chocolate?" Landon asked.

"Hot chocolate?" Eric asked.

"Yeah, Grams said in the note that there was some in the pantry, and now that I'm down here, I want it."

"Where am I supposed to put it?"

"If you can find a thermos laying around, just bring that."

"Oh, the old thermos that's always lying around in every grandma's kitchen?" Eric said, messing around with him.

"You don't have to, but she did offer the hot chocolate."

"I would like some," Avery agreed.

"Okay, I'll go back to the farmhouse. But I'm not disturbing your grandma. If I can't find a suitable container in the vicinity, I just won't worry about it."

"That's fine. Thanks for trying," Landon said. He handed Eric the portfolio. "That's amazing," he added, looking at me."

"I love it too," Avery added. "Now I want to hire Eric to come build something at my house. That's such a cool logo."

"Landon drew it," I said.

"Yeah, but whoever made those really fixed it up," Landon said. "That's good work."

"I'm taking it up to the truck," Eric said decisively. He stood and then reached down to help me up.

I gave him my hand, and he pulled me to my feet. It was darker standing, but I could still clearly see his face. There were shadows. He was gorgeous—his full lips smirking at me. We were hanging out with two other people and he couldn't kiss me, but I could tell he wanted to.

"Are we going back up?" I asked him.

"Are you okay with that?"

I nodded, and then Eric put the leather folder into his backpack and put on a jacket before shrugging into the backpack. He strapped his headlamp on, and I did the same, the jacket first and then my headlamp.

"Ready?" he asked. He reached for my hand and I gave it to him. We quickly found the path, and I followed Eric step for step. He held my hand, talking me through each turn, coaching me, saying things to reassure me. We talked about the gift and the people I had hired to design and print it.

It went much quicker without our bags and with only two people, and it seemed like no time before we made it to the ladder again.

Seeing light was such a relief. It was dark out, but compared to the cave, it was extremely bright. We came out of the shack, and the moon and the stars lit up the space around us in spite of the fact that we were in the woods. It was dark out and it was still so wonderfully bright to me.

Within a minute, we were out of the shack and heading out of the gate. Eric stayed by the gate after he closed it. He took his headband off, and he pulled me into an embrace, wrapping his arms securely around me. I took my headband off and put it in my pocket before relaxing again.

He stared at me as he held me.

"I'm glad we're getting a minute alone," I said. "I mean, it normally wouldn't matter, but I wanted to… I hadn't talked to you since that thing that happened between us in the hallway last night, and I didn't know how you felt about it. I wanted to ask you that."

"Oh, yeah, last night," he said, acting serious. "I remember that thing in the hallway, now that you mention it."

"I didn't know if you felt anything about it," I said shyly.

"Look at me, Rose."

I glanced at him, and our eyes locked. It was cold and dark and didn't mind a bit.

"I feel a lot about it," he said, causing a wave of love and relief to wash over me. "I feel all sorts of things about it."

"Are they good things?" I asked.

"I'm amazed that you have to ask that," he said. "All summer, I…" he trailed off, shaking his head.

"What? All summer you what?"

"Nothing. You were not in the same place then as you are now."

"I like where I am right now," I said referring to my proximity to him.

Eric grinned. "You mean right this second? You like freezing in the dark woods in the middle of January?"

"Is it dark and freezing? I hadn't even noticed."

I felt like I might explode into a thousand bits. His hands came up, and he held onto the sides of my face, holding me gently while my arms wrapped around his work-hardened mid-section.

He kissed me gently—his mouth barely touching mine. His kiss was scorching but patient. I was not at all aware of the cold weather because I was on fire with attraction and desire and maybe even love. Love. It had to be love. There was nothing else that felt like this. I had never felt it before. It wasn't just physical. Although the physical aspect was so amazing that my body felt like it had turned to hot lava and would surely melt.

Eric pulled back and then scanned my face, looking at me like he was amazed and couldn't believe I was standing there. "Let's go to the truck so you don't get too cold," he said.

I nodded, and he smiled at me as he turned and pulled me along.

Chapter 11

Eric and I held hands as we walked through the woods. We easily found his truck and took it back to the farmhouse. The curtains weren't drawn, and we could see Landon's great-grandmother in the kitchen window when we pulled up. We got out, and Eric knocked on the door.

She recognized him and welcomed us in, introducing herself and asking how I knew Landon and Eric. She was a large lady, both tall and broad, and dressed in a long nightgown. I instantly felt comforted and at home in her presence. She said that she would be happy to make hot chocolate and put it in a container for us, but that it would take a minute. We agreed to that, and she put some water in the kettle.

There was a small, wooden table for four in the dining area that was connected to her kitchen. Eric walked in that direction, presumably to sit down, and I followed him. "Grams, you need to come look at these business cards Rose got me for my birthday," he said.

She came over and sat at the table with us, and Eric took the portfolio out of the backpack. He set it in front of her in the closed position.

"She had my initials put on this thing, but open it and look at this stuff on the inside."

"Oh, my heavens," she said. She took some glasses off of the table and put them on so she could focus on the letterhead. "Can you turn on that light?" she asked, causing Eric to pop up and flip a nearby switch. "Oh, this is nice," she said. "Do you have your own business? Is this you, E. Jones?"

"Yes, ma'am, Eric Jones."

"Patios and Docks?"

"Yes ma'am, I build them."

"Oh, my goodness, alive. And you made these business cards?" she asked, looking at me.

"Yes, those and the folder," Eric agreed. He took them back from her when she handed them over, and he stared at them again. "We were down in the cave when she gave them to me, so I didn't really get to look at it yet. That's why I brought it in with me."

"Oh, you've already been down in the cave? I knew y'all came by the house, but I didn't know how long you had been gone. I just came downstairs a second ago."

"How long do we have to wait on the water?" Eric asked.

Grams looked at a clock and then back at Eric. "Probably five or ten minutes, why? Did you change your mind? Are you in a big hurry?"

"No ma'am, I was wondering if we have time for a round of Uno." He grabbed the card box from the center of the table, took them out, and began shuffling.

"Oh, I took that game out of the cabinet so that you and Landon could play with your friends."

"That's what I was wanting to do right now," he said. "Do you have time?"

"Lord, goodness. Me? Well, I guess I can play a round of Uno, if you wanted to do it right here at the table." She spoke slowly, and Eric was already dealing by the time she finished the sentence. "I don't know if I remember the rules to Uno," she said. "There has to be one of something, because that's what the name means."

"You need to get rid of all of your cards, but things keep happening to you, like you have to draw more cards and things like that. And when you get down to one card in your hand, you have to say Uno, or if someone catches you and says it before you, you have to draw four more. I hope you ladies are ready to fight to the finish on this, because I *do not* take it easy just because you are women." He turned over the top card and glanced at us. "I will let you go first, but I will not be taking it easy other than that."

"Well, I wanted to let you know that I've always been lucky when it comes to cards," Grams said, playing along and trying her hand at smack-talking.

"Yeah, I've been lucky with cards, too," I said, agreeing with her and warning him in a teasing tone.

For the next ten minutes, we played a fun game of Uno. Each of us got close to winning a few times, and mid-way through, we stopped to tend to the kettle, which was whistling.

Grams enjoyed playing with us, I could tell. We all had fun during the game. We finished, and I won. I was a little reluctant and sort of wanted to see Grams win, but I had the correct card at the end of the game, and we all laughed when I threw it down and Eric pitched a fake fit like it was the world championship.

Grams was still laughing as she stood up. "Oh, well, I guess I'll make your hot chocolate so you don't have to sit here and play cards with an old lady all night."

She was teasing and obviously delighted with our company, but we knew she had a routine and we only stayed long enough to finish making the hot chocolate and say goodbye to her. It felt great to know that I had a backup plan and would have a nice, welcoming house to sleep in if the dark cave didn't work out for me. For the moment, I didn't care where I was as long as E. Jones was next to me.

We drove the truck down to the trailhead toward the back of the property, and Eric thanked me again for the letterhead and told me how special it was. I was relieved that he liked it since I was worried that he might think I had taken too much liberty with the design.

The trek down into the cave was easier this time since I knew what to expect. It was surreal to find the two of them, Landon and Avery, sitting in a small dome of light when we rounded that last corner.

"That was quick," Landon said.

"I heard them coming two minutes ago," Avery said.

"We heard you guys, too," Eric said.

I followed him to the place where Avery and Landon were sitting around our 'campfire' which was a battery-operated heater and five small lanterns. I glanced at Landon and Avery, seeing their proximity, and wondering if they were more than friends or just looking cozy because they had been alone during the last hour in a gigantic system of caves.

Their casual, cozy posture made Eric take the liberty to move his mat near mine. He placed it so that it was positioned diagonally in front of mine, and he stretched out on it, lying close to me and letting his arm rest on my lap.

"I am in awe over how black the darkness is," I said, trying to seem unaffected by Eric.

"Have you seen it without lights yet?" Landon asked.

"Eric stopped on the path just now and made me turn off my headlamp."

"I'll bet he did," Landon said suggestively. "But seriously, check this out. Just stay where you are and keep your eyes wide open."

Landon stood up. First, he leaned down to where he had been sitting and turned up the speaker, which was barely audible until then. The music loudened, filling up the space in the cave.

"That speaker sounds good," Eric said, smiling as he inched closer to me, scooting my way until his head was resting in my lap. I felt warmth spread in my body, and I took off my jacket, tossing it onto my bag.

"It's my new JBL," Avery said, speaking over the music.

I didn't recognize the song, but it was classical music, which surprised me.

Landon stooped over the lanterns and one by one turned them off. "I'll turn it up a little more once I sit down," he said. "I'll leave it on for one song, and then I'll turn the lights back on."

"If it gets too dark for you, just grab a flashlight," Avery said to me.

"Oh, yeah, if you don't like it, just speak up and we'll turn the lanterns back on," Landon agreed.

I glanced down at Eric, who still had his head resting on my lap. He was halfway upside down and he peered back, gazing at me as Landon caused the cave to turn to black, one lantern at a time.

"Are you okay with it?" he asked. I nodded, smiling as I watched Landon turn off the last lantern. He still had a flashlight in his hand, otherwise he would have a hard time making it back to his mat.

"See you on the other side," Landon said.

He sat down and then turned up the music before turning off his flashlight. Sounds filled the cave and the darkness was like a cool, damp blanket resting on me. My eyes were wide open and I could see nothing but blackness. I started to feel an ounce of panic, but right then, Eric pulled on my shirt, tugging at it twice like he wanted to tell me something. I leaned down, and he put his hands around my face, pulling me down to him. He spoke near my ear, whispering.

"Are you okay?" he asked. The music was so loud that I knew there was no way the others could hear us.

"I'm fine with you right here," I answered, leaning in close to him, staying near him.

"Come lay by me," he said.

And I did. The darkness was thick, and I could not see a single thing, but I used my sense of touch and adjusted my mat so that it was next to his. Eric moved, snuggling me gently, helping me situate, and holding me close to him. His body was now resting along mine from my head to my toes, and I would have it no other way. He put his arm over me and I stayed there, snug in his embrace and taking in the surreal moment.

The music and the complete darkness had me feeling like I was in another world. I contemplated God and the vast complexities of His creation. I couldn't believe a temperature-controlled pocket existed under the surface of the earth. I couldn't believe I had left my life in Chicago and was currently in a different state and inside one of these God-made pockets.

And then I felt Eric's hand. I felt his fingers come around my jaw, gently prodding at me to bring my face closer to his. I stretched that way and could feel that my cheek was next to his, and my heart started beating out of control. I almost whispered something to him, but his lips found mine before I could find the words.

The music and the darkness completely enveloped us, and then just like that, his lips were on mine. I wasn't expecting him to kiss me, but my body knew no other response but to kiss him back. I leaned further so that I could reach him. His hand came up to my cheek, and he held me gently as he kissed me.

We connected deeply this time. He opened his mouth to me, and I kissed him like a woman kisses a man she loves. I did love Eric. I felt connected to him and it wasn't just the gut-wrenching gloriousness of his tongue against mine. It was more than that.

He kissed me for what must have been a minute or two with soft, exploring kisses.

"I'm sorry, but I love you," he said, whispering near my ear once he finally broke the kiss. The music was still loud, but there was no mistaking what he said.

"Why are you sorry?" I whispered to him.

This made him kiss me again. Oh, goodness, did he kiss me. He moved and covered me so thoroughly in his kiss that it gave me physical sensations that I didn't even know were possible. I had never felt like this before. I never wanted to kiss another man in my entire life. I wanted to stay by Eric's side forever.

"I'm turning on a light," Landon warned out of nowhere, causing me to flinch and then pull away.

It took a second for me to come back to reality.

Landon switched on his flashlight and then turned the music down.

I sat up, adjusting my hair and face and resituating in a cross-legged position while Eric stayed laying down but adjusted so that his head was in my lap again.

One-by-one, Landon turned the lanterns back on. "That's a trip, isn't it?" he asked, looking at me now that we had light.

"It's unbelievable," I said. "I'm never going to forget this for the rest of my life."

Eric moved, comfortably tucking his hand in the crease of my leg.

"I moved to Pittsburgh two years ago," Avery said. "And I still come back. I know we're growing up and we won't do this forever, so I'm in whenever Eric calls."

"How do you like Pittsburgh?" I asked, still feeling dazed and trying to get in on the conversation.

"I like it. I grew up here, but now I just come back for this trip. There's nothing like it. I've only missed a few."

"Landon, is this the only time you come out here?" I asked. "Or do you come with other people?"

"Both. I used to come out here more, but in the last few years, it's pretty much been just on Eric's birthday. It's a good weekend because it's closed, and we've just made a tradition of it."

"When we were younger, we came in one time while there was a tour going on," Eric said.

Landon laughed. "Yeah, and we dared your boyfriend to do something crazy, and he did it. He actually did it."

"You bet me a hundred bucks that I wouldn't."

"You probably would have done it for free," Landon said.

"I did do it for free," Eric said. "You never paid me."

"What did he do? What did you do?" I asked, looking at Eric.

"We snuck in during business hours, and he joined the back of the group of tourists and went through the rest of the tour with them."

"It took an hour to get out that way," Eric said. "I had to smile and wave at them all in the parking lot and then take off running about five miles in the woods to get back to Landon's family's entrance."

"And he got his Vans all muddy."

"I did have on my favorite pair of shoes, and I did get them muddy. It was not comfortable."

I was so caught up in the conversation that I blew past the boyfriend comment. But I most certainly replayed it in my mind later that night.

Chapter 12

I slept next to Eric, and it was the most comfortable, wonderful night's rest I ever had. We left a few lanterns on, and all four of us slept right next to each other—all fully clothed and under our own blankets. Avery and I slept next to each other in the middle with a wall of men around us.

I would have been frightened out of my wits if Eric hadn't been there, but with him next to me, I felt assured and confident, and I slept well. His arm was around me when I went to sleep, and I woke up to his hand rubbing my arm to rouse me.

"Good morning," Eric said.

I realized he was no longer lying next to me, but he was kneeling down next to me. He had his shoes on and was alert, and I picked up my head, feeling startled. He smiled and rubbed me comfortingly with strokes to my blanketed arm.

"I'm about to wake Avery and Landon up," he whispered. "It's eight o'clock, and we'll need to get on back."

"It's eight o'clock in the morning?" I asked, looking around, blinking, marveling at the fact that the campsite looked the exact same as it did the night before.

Landon and Avery heard Eric talking to me and they began to stir.

"Sorry," Avery moaned when she rolled over and hit me.

"It's fine," I said.

It took us ten or fifteen minutes to wake up and get packed. They walked me over to one of the underground lakes before we left. All we had were flashlights, so it was impossible for me to get the scope of everything, but it was surreal to be under so many layers of earth in a cavern so big that we could all easily and comfortably breathe and survive… and then to see bottomless water while we were down there… my brain felt like it was about to explode.

I contemplated God and wondered if He would put wonderful things like this there for us to explore. He would. I knew He would. He had made this, and Heaven would only be better. Being underground in a cave made me contemplate God and my own existence, which directly translated into a general feeling of seize-the-day-ed-ness in me.

I knew that feeling would affect my approach to Eric. He was a gem of a person, and I had to make a way to be with him. I liked him too much to keep pretending everything was normal. I liked him too much to go back to my job in Chicago and forget all of this happened.

We stopped at the farmhouse to use the restroom and return the hot chocolate container. We didn't see either of Landon's grandparents this time, so we left them a note, thanking them.

I sat in the backseat with Landon again.

We stopped at a gas station and fast food restaurant for something to eat and drink before we got on the road. It was a rural area, and we didn't have many options. I bought a pre-packaged granola bar, some coffee, and a pack of candy for the road. I balanced all of it in one hand and held Eric's hand with the other when we met up to stand in line at the register. He took my hand and smiled, looking a little surprised that I would reach out for him in public.

The surreal nature of being in that cave had changed me, and I no longer wanted to waste any time pretending that I didn't love him. I did love him, after all. He had said it to me the night before, and I hadn't returned the sentiment, but I did love him. I was pretty sure I had loved him for a long time.

We made it back to the lake house by noon.

Landon and Avery took off right away, but Eric said he was staying for a while. I didn't know how long a while was, but any time I could get with him was fine by me.

"Is today Sunday?" I asked, as Landon and Avery drove away. I knew it was. I knew I was leaving tomorrow, and it was terrible and hard to believe. "Where did the time go?" I asked, before he could answer the first question.

"Did you have fun?" he asked, reaching for my hand.

"So much fun. It's cold out here. Come in and eat some real food with me."

"Oh, are you cooking this real food?" he asked, knowing I was a simple eater who often "heated up" things, but never did much real cooking.

I shrugged. "I was thinking about making waffles. That I can do."

We both knew Uncle Max had a nice waffle iron in the kitchen, and Eric touched his stomach. "I could put down a waffle right now," he said.

"How much do I get you today?"

"I don't know what you're asking, but it's a lot, whatever you're saying."

I laughed. "I'm asking if you have to leave—if you have to work. I'm telling you that I'm already dreading tomorrow when I have to go back, and I was hoping you could stay."

"I took today off," he said.

"Does that mean you'll stay over here, maybe?"

He turned to me with a smile. "Yes, Rose, it does mean I'll stay over here." He was looking at me with a mischievous smile that had my heart racing. He knew I was acting differently after last night. He thought it was because we had kissed in the cave. And honestly, that might've added to it. It truly was glorious. But that wasn't all. I just had a general sense of never wanting to leave his side, ever again.

I was about to say something else to him when my brother came outside, opening the door and suddenly appearing a few feet from us.

"Hey, Beau," I said.

By instinct, I straightened, leaning away from Eric. But then I realized I didn't want to do that any longer, and I reached out and took Eric's hand again.

"We just got back," I said, standing casually.

"I was coming out to see if you guys wanted lunch," he said. "We have some chicken in there. I was going to fire up the grill."

"What about fried chicken?" I asked. "I was going to make waffles. What if we had fried chicken and waffles?" I turned and looked at Eric. "Is that too much?"

"I've never fried chicken," Beau said as a disclaimer. "Holland might know how to do it."

"I know how to fry chicken," Eric said.

"Well, that sounds good to me. I know we have a bunch of stuff in there because Holland just went to Little Rock grocery shopping. You guys can make lunch, and I'll just eat it. Is that okay?"

We spent the next hour preparing food for the four of us. We made extra because we weren't the only ones in the house and left-over food always disappeared from the fridge.

Beau and Holland sat and ate lunch with us, and we told them about the cave experience. We told them about the darkness and playing Uno, and then about the midnight trip to the woods to use the restroom before we all went to sleep. I was delirious during that trek, and I slipped several times even though I really was trying to concentrate on my footing. We laughed as we recalled various details of the camping trip to my brother and his wife.

He told them about the letterhead and Eric even went out to his truck to get it so that they could take a look. We told them a lot, but we didn't dare mention the experience of darkness with music and bliss.

We spent the early part of the afternoon with Beau and Holland, and then later, Uncle Max and Casey showed up and we all sat around the living room and talked. It was getting close to dinner time and we had just discussed eating again when I excused myself to use the restroom. I went to my bedroom since I had a bathroom in there with all of my things.

I came out to a male presence in my room. I assumed it would be Eric coming in there to get a minute alone, but it was my brother.

"Hey, Beau," I said, coming out of the bathroom and looking at him with a curious expression.

"Did mom tell you he's not good enough for you?"

"What? Who? What are you talking about?" I pretended to be confused because his words instantly struck a chord.

"You. Eric. Why are you so obsessed with making us all think he's a success?"

"What? I'm not."

"Yes, you are. You keep talking him up, but we already like him. What's your problem? Did Mom tell you not to go out with him?"

"Not in those exact words, and it's been a long time since we had that conversation."

"Well, it must still be sticking with you because you keep trying to talk us into liking Eric and it's not necessary. We already like him. I don't need to know that his business is succeeding and he's booked until next summer. I like the regular Eric just fine."

I took a deep breath. "I like the regular Eric fine, too. I don't know what I'm gonna do, Beau."

"What do you mean?"

"I think I love him. I do love him. I don't want to go home. I'm freaking out that I have to leave tomorrow. I feel like I'm going to break down and cry about it right now."

"Don't cry," he said instantly. "Just come back in the summer and come stay a few weeks like last summer. Holland and I will still be here. It would be amazing."

"I don't have a few weeks. This job is too new for that. I get a week, and that's unpaid. Right now, I'm here on sick days."

"Well, come back and stay for a week in the summer. That's right around the corner. And maybe you guys can drive and meet in the middle between now and then. I think it's just four or five hours if you want to drop everything one weekend. Maybe in St. Louis."

I stared straight ahead. Technically, I was looking at the rug, but I wasn't seeing anything. I was lost in thought.

"That's easy for you to say, Beau. But you don't... how would you feel if Holland had to stay here while you went back to Chicago for work?"

My brother pulled back and looked at me with a long, appraising stare. "Are you comparing yourself and Eric to me and Holland right now?"

"Yes," I said, without flinching.

"You... like him... that much?" His face was a mask of confusion.

"You look like this is all sudden. I've had a thing for him for a long time."

"Does Mom not like him?"

"No, she doesn't. She told me I can do better."

"She didn't like Holland either. Nobody's good enough for her kids."

"Charles was good enough," I said.

"Charles wasn't as good as Eric," Beau replied.

"I know. I love him, Beau. I don't know what to do about going back. I feel sick about it. I want to call in sick for the rest of my life."

He breathed a sigh. "Oh, my gosh, Rose, I had no idea. Does he feel like that?"

"Yes. I think. I'm pretty sure. We're just now starting to say that kind of stuff, but yes. He said he does."

"He said he loves you?"

"Yes."

"Did you say it back?"

"We didn't have time. I didn't have time." I reached out and held my brother's hand. "What am I going to do?" I asked.

He shook his head. "I don't know. I don't know how to answer that. That's something you have to figure out for yourself."

Chapter 13

Eric took some time off to spend the weekend with me. He had jobs planned, so he had to go back on Monday. He spent the early morning with me, and he left at 10am knowing it was the last time I would see him for a while.

It was difficult for both of us. We didn't have much privacy this weekend, but when we were alone, we connected in ways that made leaving simply terrible.

"Bye, Holland," I said, finding her and her little dog, Ralphie, in the living room when I finished getting ready.

"Are you leaving already?"

"Yeah, I just texted Beau and he's coming to get me a few minutes early. We're going by Eric's job site. I just said goodbye to him a little while ago, but I want to go by there. I just want to see him one more time. I texted Beau, and he said he'd take me over there."

"Oh, good." She stood up and hugged me. "I barely got to see you on this trip, and I'm going to miss having you around."

"I'll miss you too. It's hard to imagine that tomorrow at this time, I'll be in my office at work."

"You sound… not that excited."

"It was too short this time," I said, thinking of Eric. My heart was broken into about a trillion unhealable pieces at the thought of leaving him. The only thing that could make it better was not leaving him.

I faked a smile and hugged my sister-in-law.

"I'm taking Rose to the airport," my brother said coming inside.

"That's what she was just saying," Holland replied.

And within a few minutes, we were on the road. The house where Eric was working was ten minutes from the lake house, and not necessarily on the way to the airport. But Beau was really nice about it and didn't mention the fact that I had already said goodbye to Eric that morning.

My brother said he'd wait in the truck when we pulled up at the place where Eric was working. I knew where it was because it was a prominent house on the lake and I had seen it from a boat before. Eric had explained to me what house he was working on, and I was familiar with the place.

"I'll wait here," Beau said.

"I'll just be a minute. I wanted to say one thing."

"That's fine, I'm not in a hurry," he said, tilting his seat back like he expected to be there a while.

"Thanks Beau," I said, closing the door. I didn't knock on the front door of the house. I just walked around to the back, knowing they would be outside. I walked past Eric's truck and other vehicles in the driveway, and I headed toward the back of the house. I stared down, huddled against the January wind, concentrating on every step and noticing the thick blades of grass under my feet. It was a gorgeous home, similar to, though not as large as my uncle's place.

I had tried to text Eric from the road, but he only checked his phone every couple of hours when he was working.

I came around the back of the house to find Zack, Landon's younger brother, carrying wood. I knew who it was because I had seen his picture. "Oh, hey," he said, looking at me like I wasn't who he expected to see.

"I'm Rose Cameron. I'm here to see Eric."

"Oh, Rose?" he said with wide eyes. He had been holding two long boards, and he instantly but carefully dropped them down. "I'll come back for these. Let me show you where Eric is. We have to keep the saw over here so we don't get sawdust in their swimming pool."

"Oh," I said, nodding. I followed him absentmindedly, thinking about what I was going to say to Eric.

"How did you like the cave?" he asked.

"Amazing. Like nothing I've ever done before. Oh, hey," I added, rounding another corner and seeing Eric.

"Hey," he said. he straightened, looking concerned. "You okay?"

I nodded. "I just wanted to tell you something for a second before I head to the airport."

Eric had been standing with his feet on the ground. The working surface of the deck was a few feet higher than that and Eric sprang up, hopping onto it before heading my way. He shed his gloves and tossed them to the side, walking on the section of deck that was complete.

"This looks so good," I said, taking it all in. I pulled out my phone. "Can I get a photo while it's under construction?"

"Of course, he said.

"Hang on, don't keep walking. I want you in it."

Eric paused and smiled, and I snapped a photograph. I stared at it for a second knowing that it would make me ache for him later. I stashed the phone in my pocket and smiled at him, reaching for his hand. Zack had left us alone, but he passed us again, carrying the boards.

"Just line them up on the grass right there. I'll get to it when I'm done with Rose. Thank you, Zack."

"No problem," Zack said with a nod.

We took off walking around the side of the house, away from Zack and the wood he was carrying. We stopped when we were on the far side of the house with no one around. I could see the lake in the background, but I wasn't even concerned with my surroundings.

"What is it?" he asked as we came to a stop. He leaned against the house and pulled me against him.

It was cold out, but it was warmer with the shelter of the house right next to us.

"I love you," I said quietly. "I didn't say it, and then I regretted it, so I didn't want to get on a plane before I came here and—"

He kissed me. He leaned down and placed a slow, patient, warm kiss on my mouth.

I stretched upward toward him. "I love you," I repeated, whispering.

"I love you, too, Rose. I don't deserve your love, but I love you, too."

"What do you mean by that? It's so untrue."

"It's not about money or power, that's not what I'm saying. I'm saying I don't deserve you because of choices I've made. I felt you stiffen next to me when your brother brought up Nashville."

"I'm sorry. I don't mean to stiffen up."

"You shouldn't be sorry. I'm the one who's sorry. I made that choice in my past, and now I have consequences. But all I can do is be the best man I can possibly be and hope that we can go past it."

"We can go past it," I said. "We are past it."

"How far past it?" he asked.

"I know you still have friends there, and I'm fine with it. I want to meet them."

"I wasn't talking about Nashville anymore. I'm asking about me and you. How far will we go?"

His voice was slow and deep and he pulled me closer to him. I leaned in. "I'm not sure that I have any limits with you, Eric."

"I want to be together, Rose," he said, looking down at me until I made eye contact with him. "I only want to be with you, and I want it all the time. I wish you were waiting for me when I get home this afternoon. I don't want you to leave."

I took a deep breath, and he hugged me, holding me close to him. He smelled like fresh-cut wood, and I held him like my life depended on it.

"I don't want to leave, either," I said. "I want you. I want to stay with you."

He breathed out a long sigh at the horrible thought of goodbye.

We just stood there and held each other in a tight embrace for a full minute, maybe two. "I don't know what to say," he said.

"Say goodbye for now," I said. "I have to go back. I'm on my way right now. Beau's waiting for me in the driveway." I looked up after I said it, and he leaned down and kissed me. His mouth came to mine, and I leaned in pressing upward, kissing him back. He loved me, and he showed me that by the way he touched me and looked at me. He held the sides of my face, kissing me, loving on me like I was the absolute center of his world.

"I love you," he said. I nodded. Silent tears fell down my face, and he saw them and pulled back, looking at me like he was concerned for me.

"I love you, too," I said. I wiped at my tears. "I'm fine. Don't look at this. I'm just sad about leaving."

"I'm sad about you leaving too, my girl. I don't want you to go. But I know you have to. We're going to figure it out, okay? Even if I have to go to Chicago to see you."

"Yeah, and St. Louis is halfway," I added, trying not to gasp. "But I would love to come up with a… " I trailed off, feeling shy and stopping myself mid-sentence.

"Come up with a what?"

"Nothing."

"What? What were you going to say?"

"Nothing. I'm not saying it."

"You have to." He squeezed me. "Say it."

"I would love to come up with a… more… perm…a… nent… solution."

"Yessss," he said, pulling on me, holding me greedily, shaking me in his arms.

I laughed.

"Yes, ma'am. That's what I'm talking about. I would love for you to come up with a permanent solution. No more leaving. Let's figure out how to do that, okay?" He smiled at me, and his face was simply irresistible. I thought of him on his skateboard—the rough, nonchalant rockstar. He was wild, and I stared at him realizing that I was the one he wanted. It made me weak in the knees.

"Okay well, that's all I have to say. That's what I came by here to say… that I love you and that I want to find a way to not do this goodbye thing anymore if possible."

"Those are the two best things you could've possibly said. I agree wholeheartedly, and I love you, too, Rosie."

Chapter 14

Eric

How in the world was he expecting to go back to his normal life? He couldn't. He had been touched, changed. Rose had come into his life in a capacity where she was more than his friend, and Eric would never be the same because of it. He had just gotten his life together to a point where he was working on a real goal, and now he felt topsy-turvy and willing to scrap the whole idea and start over.

He would happily do that if it meant he could be next to her. Eric thought about it all day, and he realized that there was no way he could stay in Arkansas while Rose Cameron lived in Chicago. He could not stand it. Several times throughout the day, he almost left the job and went straight to the airport.

His heart ached. His stomach hurt. He had barely eaten all day. He worked until sunset, and then he tried to call his girl on the way home, but he couldn't reach her.

He got a call from her brother later that evening saying that Rose had dropped her phone into a toilet at the airport and had lost everything. She was in the process of getting a new phone, but she wouldn't be able to talk to him until the following day.

Eric was happy to know she was safe, and he knew it was just a phone, but he worried about her. He was tortured waiting to talk to her. He had no idea how he had gone his whole life without having her in his life. He checked his work email later that evening, and he blinked when he saw Rose's name.

There was a video, and he clicked on it instantly, turning his phone to try to make her show up larger on the screen. It was framed at the desk in her bedroom. He could see things in the background, but he concentrated on Rose. She had her hair in a ponytail with no makeup on.

"Hi," she said, waving at the camera. He covered his mouth with his fist, hardly able to watch. He wanted to be with her to the point that it hurt. "It's been quite a day. I sat down to write you an email, and I thought it would take forever to explain everything, but I couldn't call with no phone… so anyway, I'm making a video." She breathed a sigh, smiling a tired smile as she focused on the screen. "My phone fell into a toilet, first of all, which is gross. So gross. It was basically right when I went to the airport. It was in Little Rock where it happened. It fell out of my back pocket, and I swear I will never hold my phone back there again." She couldn't help but smile as she looked down, remembering the incident. "It was so disgusting, and I had to reach into… anyway, I rinsed my phone and then wiped it with a wipe, and by the time I did all that, it didn't work. It wouldn't turn on. I haven't taken it to the phone shop yet because they were closed by the time my flight landed and I was able to get to the store." She looked at the camera with a smile, and Eric felt like he wanted to jump through the phone. "I can't believe I was in Arkansas this morning and now I'm setting my alarm to wake up for work. I'll be there all day tomorrow. I have some things to catch up on. I'm going to try to use my lunch break to see about getting a new phone. Hopefully, I'll be able to call you then. If you're working, I'll just leave you a message. Eric, I miss you already. I'm thinking about this weekend and the cave..." she trailed off and paused, staring at the camera. Eric could hardly contain himself. "I miss you. I miss being next to you. I'm here and I'm fine, and the flight was good and everything. No turbulence. Technically, everything is going good. But I miss you, Eric. I should have stayed longer. I want you to know that I'm proud of you, though. I'm happy that you're working for yourself, and I'm really proud. I think you're already the coolest guy in the whole world, and now you're going to have a big, successful business. I'm really proud of you. I didn't get to tell you that. You wanted something and you went after it. You're amazing and inspiring." She sighed. "Anyway, I just wanted to update you about my phone and tell you I miss you so much. I really do. I might be able to give you a call tomorrow at lunch, but don't worry if it's tomorrow night. Anyway, I love you. Thank you for letting me experience this weekend with you." She stopped talking and blew a smiling kiss, waving to the camera before reaching out to turn it off.

Eric was fuming.

He was on fire.

There was way, way, way, way, way too much space between himself and Rose Cameron. He wanted her next to him, in the same room, her skin pressed up next to his. He wanted to smell her perfume and see her smile at him. He wished he could reach out for her right then.

Chicago.

Chicago was a fine city.

Eric watched the video again, and just after it finished, he placed a phone call.

"Hello?" Max Morgan answered the phone on the first ring. "Everything all right, Eric?"

"Yes, sir. I was just wondering if I could talk to you for a minute."

"You sure can. You can always talk to me, but especially now. I'm on the road for another hour."

"Oh, are you in Little Rock?"

"No, I'm in France."

"In France?"

"Yes," Max said.

Eric hesitated, but he didn't ask any other questions. Max and Casey were travelers, and no one asked. "I'm calling because I'm trying to build my life into something respectable, and I value your opinion."

"Whoa, Eric, this is deeper than I thought. Let me turn down the radio. Okay, what now? I'm alone. You're good."

Eric breathed a sigh. "I haven't even told my dad. People know I like her, but this would probably come as a surprise to everyone. My dad has so been pushing for this dock company dream of mine, that I know he would be let down if I left and—"

"What?" Max said. "I missed something. Are you talking about quitting your business?"

"Maybe. I don't know. I might have to move."

"Move where? Oh, Chicago? Is this about Rose?"

"Yes, it is. And I've made far more regrettable decisions for far less reasons in my life. I love this business, and I'm enjoying building it and seeing it grow, but quite frankly, I'll just start over somewhere else. Who cares about the business if I'm in a constant state of crawling out of my skin?"

"Is that how you feel right now? You're crawling out of your skin?"

"Yes. I am. I do not want to be here right now."

"You do realize that you're saying all this to a divorced man."

"Yes sir, I do realize that. I knew my dad would tell me to stay in Arkansas, and I figured you would pretty much tell me the same thing."

"Then maybe that's what you want to hear. Maybe you want to hear that you should stay and focus on your business."

"I don't want to hear that. I want to hear your true, good reaction. As far as I'm concerned, I'm over it. I can just get out of my lease and start over in Chicago. I will find something to do there. Rose would love to get a job at a big newspaper. She needs a big city."

"She said that?"

"Not in so many words but she needs a column similar to the one she did in college. She's good at that. Plus, her family's there."

"Last time I checked, her brother lived at my house in Arkansas."

"He does, but everything else is in Chicago. I'm just saying… maybe I was hoping you would talk me out of it, because I feel like I'm on the verge of leaving."

"I'm not."

"You're not what?"

"I'm not going to try to talk you out of it, " Max said. "I don't believe in marriage for myself, but it's good for the right people. I think my son's better off with your sister."

"You think I should marry Rose?" Eric asked, feeling oddly excited.

Max laughed. "No, I don't. I'm not saying that. I'm just saying that I stand behind that inner rebel or whoever it is inside of you who's about to run off and start over for love."

"You stand behind that?" Eric asked, feeling astonished.

"I actually do. I think you're good for Rose, and if you love each other, then you can build decks in any city in the world. All you need is a saw and a hammer."

"I know. And I know you're right. I just can't believe it. I thought you would tell me to stay."

"Then maybe you want to stay. No offense to Chicago, but Arkansas is, quite frankly, better."

Eric laughed.

"No," Max continued. "Astrid and Danny have been up there a long time. They love it. You would have in-laws and they know a lot of people. They could maybe help get you started with another business."

"I did not expect you to say this. But, no, I'm not counting on her parents. I don't think Astrid even likes me."

"She's a tough nut," Max said. "I know since she's my sister. She'll come around. She'll do right."

"Thank you. I'm really glad I called you."

"Good. Call me anytime."

"I'm sorry I caught you in France."

"I'm not sorry. It was nice talking to you, Eric."

"I feel good now. Thank you."

"I'm honored and happy that you thought to call me with this. We only have one shot at this life. You would regret it if you didn't do everything in your power to keep this one."

Chapter 15

Rose

I took an early lunch break the following day. I went to the phone store, and I was finished before noon. They were able to recover some of my information but not all of it.

Eric's number was no longer in my phone. I had lost over half of my contacts, and he was one of them. I felt disconnected without my phone, and Eric was the first person I wanted to reach out to. I knew he was working, but I was desperate to have his number in my phone again. I had my brother's number, and I texted him from the parking lot of the Apple store, knowing he had Eric's number.

Me:
Hey, I lost my phone and most of my contacts, and now I'm just getting a new one. I need Eric Jones's number. Can you forward it to me, please?

I sat in my car at the cell phone place, hoping my brother would respond so that I could talk to Eric on my way back to work.

I didn't hear back from my brother right away, so I copied the text and pasted it to send to my uncle Max.

Me:
Hey, I lost my phone and most of my contacts, and now I'm just getting a new one. I need Eric Jones's number. Can you forward it to me, please?

It was not even a minute later when my phone rang, and I saw that it was my uncle calling.

"Hey, Uncle Max," I said, picking up the phone. "Are you at the lake house?"

"No, I'm not. I'm overseas, in France."

"Oh, wow, I'm sorry."

"No, I actually talked to Eric last night. Is your phone broken?"

"Yes."

"Well, he wants to go to Chicago."

"What?" I asked, choking.

"I talked to him last night, and he's planning on going there for you. Have you talked to him since then?"

"No, I haven't. My phone has been broken. My heart is pounding right now, Uncle Max. Are you serious? Did you talk to Eric? Eric Jones?"

"Yes, Eric Jones, and I think he loves you."

I had to hold in a squeal. I missed Eric, and the thought of him talking to my uncle about me sent a shiver of delight up my spine. I pictured Eric and I felt like I could hardly breathe.

"I have to call him!" I said.

"You really should," Uncle Max said, laughing at my enthusiasm.

"Please send me his number," I said.

"I'm texting it now."

"Thanks, Uncle Max."

My body was absolutely buzzing.

I shook as I hung up the phone.

Uncle Max sent the number, and I texted him a quick reply to thank him before pressing the buttons to call Eric. I took off in my car as it rang since I had to leave right then to get back to work.

Something picked up, but it was his voicemail.

Before I knew what was happening, the phone beeped and I was leaving a message. Pulling out into traffic was distracting, but I did my best to focus on touching base with Eric.

"Hey! Oh, my goodness, it feels so good to be able to call you. I had to get a new phone just now. I'm just leaving the store. I had to drive all the way over to the one on Michigan Avenue, so I'm on the road headed back to work. I miss you, Eric. I've been playing catch up since I've been back, and my mind just keeps going back to Arkansas."

I thought about saying that I had talked to Uncle Max and knew that Eric was thinking about coming to me but then I decided not to say it. This resulted in a pause on the voicemail. It was during this pause when I heard my phone beeping.

I glanced down at the screen and saw that Eric was calling in.

"Oh, my goodness, please, help me answer this," I said out loud to no one in particular. I didn't care that his voicemail was still recording. I fumbled for my phone, trying not to look at it, but knowing I had to in order to switch lines.

I did it. Finally. I found the button and pressed it, hoping to hear his voice as I concentrated on the busy streets in front of me.

"Hello?" I said. "Hello?"

"Hey, Rose, are you there?"

"Yes, I'm in my car and you're on the speaker. I'm alone. I'm in traffic, but I'm alone in my car. I just left the phone store."

"Rose. I need you," he said.

My heart felt like it was going to burst. "I need you too," I said, but he was already in the process of talking again.

"I'm happy and glad that you're proud of me and everything, but I'm still that stubborn, rebellious boy you first met. Nobody's going to tell me what to do. I don't have to stay here. If you want me to, I'll leave everything I've started, and I'll start over. I can do it again."

"I just talked to my uncle, and he said something about that," I said. "I don't know, Eric. I feel like if we're far enough along to think about rearranging our lives, then I could possibly go where you are instead of you coming here. At least for now. We can work on your thing, and then eventually if we want to move, we can see what to do another time. I don't know. I'm just saying. I don't think you should just pick up and… but believe me, I want you to pick up and come here, Eric. When my uncle said you had mentioned it, my heart. Believe me, I want you here. I'm just saying… it got me thinking. Let's think about it for a second in case keeping your business is the right thing to do for now."

"Well, does that mean you're coming here, then?" he asked in a matter-of-fact tone. "Because either I'm going there or you're coming here. I feel like I can't breathe right until… I just feel like one of those two options has to happen."

"I agree," I said. "I miss you and I need you. Chicago's empty. There's nothing here for me, Eric. I have a job and an apartment, and a life, and it all feels empty since I've been back. I'm like *what am I doing,* sitting here in traffic to go sit in a cube for the rest of the day."

"I'm going through the same thing. I'm trying to build a deck over here, and I don't even care about it. I'm doing it right, but dang it, Rose. My goals, this business, it's great, and I'm happy with my work, but I can do this anywhere. I'll start over. Being close to you is more important to me."

I breathed a sigh of relief at the sound of those words. I really wanted to hear him say that he wanted to be near me. I felt lonely and heartbroken without him.

"Let's think about it," I said. "Don't go quitting right now. I have my phone back, so I'll be able to call you tonight after work. We can talk more and think about what the next step should be."

"Okay. I just feel better knowing we're on the same page."

"We definitely are," I said. "We just need to talk and plan and try to figure out what's best for both of us. I might want to go there."

"Okay good, but just know that I will leave everything."

"It makes me so happy to hear you say that," I said. I was unable to hide the smile in my voice. "Seriously, Eric. I've just gone through the last two days with my head in the sand. I miss you. I need you. Maybe we can try to do something permanent by summer."

"Summer? That's forever."

"Spring?" I said.

"I was hoping for tomorrow, but yeah, spring's good."

I laughed, feeling delighted. "I want it to be tomorrow, too, but we live in different states. I have a whole apartment over here with a lease and furniture and a car and a job."

"You don't have to leave it. I'll come to you if you need me to."

"No," I said, feeling like I wanted to go to him. "Let's think about it. I have to focus on a few things at work today, but I'm off and back home by six. I'll call you."

"Okay. Zack's looking at me like he has a question. I'll let you go for now and talk to you tonight."

"Okay, love you," I said.

It felt surreal to say it so confidently.

"I love you. I'll talk to you tonight."

I hung up the phone and called my mom. I happened to be stopped at a red light, so it was easy for me to call her. It was one of the few numbers my phone hadn't lost.

"Hello? Rose? Did you get your new phone?"

"Yes, I did."

"When? Today?"

"Yes, just now. I took an early lunch break, and now I'm headed back to the office."

"Okay, well, good."

"I don't have everyone's number. I think I'm going to need you to send me some contacts."

"Okay, just text me who you're missing and I'll send them to you when I get the chance."

I could tell my mom was being matter-of-fact and somewhat distracted, so I added. "Also, I might go ahead and quit my job and move to Arkansas for a little while."

"What?"

"Yes."

"What did you say?"

My mother already sounded condescending, and my heart began to ache in the familiar, anxious, scrambling feeling I always got when I was disappointing her.

"I know this is not about that Jones boy."

"Yes, it is. It's entirely about him, Mother."

"Well, no."

"No?"

"No, Rose. I'm demanding that you don't date him."

"Uh, no."

"Take a second and think about your future. Think about your life. Imagine a wedding. You're my only daughter, Rose. We'll have a grand wedding, and who will show up? Paul and his ex-wife, Hope and Charlie, and fifty skateboarders, graffiti artists, maybe? Perhaps you could have circus acts."

"Mom, stop." My tone was serious, impassive, and she was quiet for a few seconds.

"You should not go to Arkansas," she said. "I should have stopped you from going down there last weekend. I should've known what you were doing."

"Mom, thank you for your concern, but I just want to let you know that I am serious about Eric."

"You're really not, though, Rose. You can't be. You don't even know him."

"I know him, Mom. It's you who doesn't know him."

"Listen, just take a few days to think about it. Don't make any irrational decisions."

"I won't," I lied. "But I want you to know that I really do like him, Mom. And I don't care about a wedding."

"You really do like him?" she said in an exaggerated tone that made me feel a rush of embarrassment. "You really do, Rose? Listen to yourself. And how can you not want a nice wedding? That's every girl's dream, and your father and I can provide it for you. It's our dream to do that."

"Well, I…"

"Just don't make any decisions while you're emotional. Call me after work, and we'll talk again."

"Okay."

Chapter 16

I thought about it for the rest of the afternoon, and all I kept thinking was how I badly needed to go to Arkansas—how I simply had to be with Eric. I felt sad and hopeless at the thought of staying in Chicago, and happy and hopeful at the thought of moving to Arkansas. There was tangible relief present in my body when I imagined going there. I could see myself building a life with him. I knew I would be welcomed there and protected by Eric. My heart felt tugged to go to him, and honestly, I didn't care what my mother said. Nothing in my life had ever felt so right.

I was busy at work, so the afternoon went by quickly. It was six o'clock when I called Eric. He was driving home from a job and was on the road the whole time we were talking. I was at home for a while, but then my mom texted me and said I could go eat dinner with them. Eric had some paperwork to do, so he told me he would talk to me later that evening once I was done at my parents' house.

I did not expect the next few hours to go the way they did. My mom invited me for dinner, saying she was ordering from my favorite Mexican restaurant and that she would buy enough for me to have leftovers. I should have known it was a trick. It was basically an intervention. My dad was there, and they had a big, planned intervention-type talk with me.

They had three entire binders worth of pictures set out—photos of their engagement and wedding, and then some of me being born. My mom even brought out some more recent pictures of me and ex-boyfriends. It was an ambush, and I was too kind of a daughter to storm out of there like I should have done. I just sat and listened to them, let them say their peace, nodding as if I would actually take their advice.

I was utterly bombarded. My mom had influenced my dad, and they were convinced that running off to Arkansas to be with Eric was the most fool-hardy thing I could ever, ever do. They looked at it with the same level of disdain as if I were a drug addict. The thought of me choosing Eric Jones as a boyfriend/mate/spouse was actually offensive to them. They made it clear that I would be letting them down on so many levels if I chose to pursue Eric.

I endured over an hour of this. It was heartbreaking. I just took it all in and didn't fight with them, but it hadn't been worth the food. In fact, I had barely eaten any of my food, and I didn't take any with me when I left. I didn't cry. I didn't react. I didn't argue with them. I just listened to them inundate me with their beliefs that Eric was essentially beneath our family. 'Not that we're stuck up or think we're better than anybody, but you can't ignore those things when it comes to choosing a spouse.'

My mom had called my uncle that afternoon while I was at work, and he told her that we seemed to really love each other. That set her off. By the time I got to her house, she was ready and aimed at me with a machine-gun-style verbal assault.

I left there feeling more deflated than I had in my whole life. I hated disappointing my parents, and I had done a lot over the years to keep from doing so. I loved my parents. I respected them and thought they were good people. But they were dead wrong about this, and it was heartbreaking. I knew that I would ultimately be forced to choose between my parents and Eric, and it made for the worst evening of my life.

I was home by nine o'clock, but Eric hadn't called. I was relieved by that. It wasn't that I didn't want to talk to him. I just didn't feel like talking to anyone. I had been verbally put into my place by my mother, and her fervor against Eric was so disappointing that it put me in a melancholy mood. I was glad that Eric was late calling because I wanted to try to shake it off before I talked to him.

I went ahead and took a shower when I got home. I wasn't planning on washing my hair but it felt good to get completely clean after an evening like this. I hated to disappoint my mother, but I was going to have to do just that. Even in the midst of all these terrible desperate feelings, even with all the memory books and wedding pictures, all I wanted was Eric. I thought about starting a life with Eric, and then I tried to think about other options. I really did try to imagine myself with other people. I thought of things like marrying a doctor or a lawyer or someone famous. I thought of all the things my mom would want. I tried to picture myself in those situations just to make sure my vision wasn't clouded. But it wasn't. All I wanted was Eric. I thought God wanted us to be together, too.

I wished that I was still in Arkansas right now so that I wouldn't have had to endure that dinner conversation at my mother's house. It did not accomplish what she set out for it to accomplish. It did not make me want to be with Eric any less. The only thing that it accomplished was that I now felt disappointed and hurt by my parents.

I was alone. I had one brother in Arkansas and the other was away at college at Notre Dame. I had friends in Chicago, but I felt so very alone in my apartment. My parents had told me where they stood, and I knew that I would soon be going against them. There was nothing left for me in Chicago, and that made me feel desperately sad and oddly free at the same time.

My mind was busy contemplating all of this, so I hardly noticed how late it was. I blinked at the clock, wondering why I hadn't heard from Eric yet. I called him.

"Hey," he said, picking up the phone.

"Hey," I returned.

"It's late," he said.

"I know. I just realized what time it was. I got home from my mom's and took a shower, and I've just been zoning out."

"Zoning out?"

"Yeah," I said, still feeling distracted. "Thinking about everything."

"Did you change your mind?"

"About what?" I asked.

"I don't know. Everything. Me?"

"You, Eric, I did not change my mind about. Other things I probably did."

"Like what?" he asked.

"I don't know," I said with a sigh. "Everything. I was already thinking about you and us, and then I went to my parents' house, and my mom was in a talkative mood, and not in the best mood, so I'm just…" I took another deep breath. "I wish you were here."

"I am here," he said.

"I mean here, in my living room."

"I know what you mean, and I am here. I'm almost there. I'm not in your living room yet, but almost. I've already parked, and I'm headed to your building."

My heart almost jumped out of my chest. "Are you joking?" I asked, even though it did not sound like he was joking.

"I'm not. I promise, I'm not. I'm walking into the… " He hesitated, and I heard shuffling on the phone. "Is it the third floor?"

"Yes, Eric, I'm on the third floor. Are you at my building right now? Be serious. I'm freaking out. You're making me think you're actually in Chicago, Illinois right now, and I'm—"

I sprang to my feet.

"I am in Chicago, Illinois right now. I'm on the sidewalk, walking into your building. It's freezing out here, too, Rose. How do you live like this?"

"I don't know ho-ho-wwww," I sobbed comically. "Are you really here? I'm flipping out. How would that even be possible? Did you fly here?"

"No, I got in my truck right after I talked to you earlier, and I've been driving since. I'll get back on the road again tomorrow, but yes, Rose. I had to see you. The jobs can wait."

"Are you here?"

"Yes. I'm in your building. Thank goodness. It's warm in here."

"Oh, Eric, you are… oh, my gosh, I… I'm… Are you in my apartment building, for sure?"

"Yes. For sure. I have your address, and I put it in my GPS. I've been headed here for the past nine hours. Two short stops, food, gas, coffee, restroom, and here we are, headed up to the third floor."

"Oh, I am the happiest person in the whole world right now. Wait? You're headed up? I'm coming to you. I'm headed down there."

"Oh, no, I'm already headed up."

"How? What?" I asked, thinking that couldn't be right.

"Yes. I was walking in next to a nice lady, and she overheard our conversation. She offered me a ride up."

"I live on the eighth floor," the lady said, still hearing him.

I was already in the elevator by this time. The door had closed, and I began pushing buttons to try to get them to open back up.

"Stay on my floor," I said when I felt myself moving downward. "Stay on the third floor. Don't come back downstairs. I'm almost in the lobby now, and I'm headed back up to you as soon as I get there."

"Thank you," Eric said.

"You're welcome," I said by instinct. But then I heard a dinging noise and I realized he was talking to the lady who had let him inside.

"I'm here, Rose," Eric said a few seconds later.

Meanwhile, my elevator finalllllllly made it to the ground floor. I pressed the button to go to the third floor and then quickly pressed the 'close door' button. I pushed it several times, rushing it along.

The doors closed ever so slowly.

"How in the world did you make it upstairs so fast?" I asked him.

"I don't know. But I'm going to stand here by the elevators and wait for you. I'm hanging up. I'll see you in a second, and we won't need phones between us."

"Okay," I said. "Love you, bye."

I spoke quickly and then hung up.

I pressed the elevator button again, just to encourage it to get a move on and take me to the third floor. I stared at my reflection in the mirrored walls. I was freshly showered and had on pajamas, and I didn't even think of that or consider what I was wearing. I rode upward, feeling like I wanted to jump out of this elevator and climb the walls to get upstairs. *Was he at my apartment? Was this real? Could this be?* I tried to remember when I had talked to him on my lunch break. *I should have taken the stairs. I could have certainly climbed faster than this.*

The elevator was taking way too long.

But then the door opened, and the wave of relief hit me when I laid eyes on him.

There he was. Eric Jones.

He was standing in front of me.

Eric, in the flesh, on my floor, in my hallway.

Arkansas must have been a gigantic place, because he seemed too big for Chicago, too big for my apartment building. I took the few steps and fell

into his arms. Eric caught me, turning and swinging
me to the side to lessen the force.

Chapter 17

Eric. Eric. Eric. I was suddenly unexpectedly in his arms, and yes, yes, oh, my ever loving goodness, yes! It was right. This was sooo good. I squeezed him and held him, trying not to cry even though it was almost impossible. My eyes stung and I felt like I might physically explode with excitement. He leaned down and kissed me, and I kissed him back, feeling like I could die a happy woman in this moment.

"Your lips taste like blue raspberry," I said, pulling back, wiping a tear that had escaped out of the back corner of my eye. "I'm in heaven, and it tastes like candy."

"It's some mint thing I was eating a minute ago. I got it at a gas station."

"Oh, my gosh," I said, blinking at him, pulling back to focus on him. "You said words. You're real. You're not a dream. Tell me you ate candy again."

"What?"

"Tell me again about the mint and the gas station. I want to hear you talking, so I can believe you're here, Eric."

"I'm holding you," he said. "If I weren't here, you'd fall over." He grinned. "And I ate candy. It was ice breakers or ice berry, something with *ice* in the name."

"Mm," I said, licking my lips. "No wonder it tastes good. Come here. Come in. I'm over here," I took his hand and pulled him down the hall. "Do you have anything? A bag?"

"No," he said with a laugh.

We walked into my apartment and he looked around for a second. "It's the same as FaceTime and yet totally different being here. You told me how small it was, so it seems bigger than I expected."

"Oh, good," I said. "I was just thinking the opposite about you. You're so much smaller in my uncle's house. Come in. Come sit on the couch."

"I would love to, but I could use a quick shower, Rose." He looked down at his own clothes—those classic dark khaki working man pants with a long sleeve thermal shirt layered with a thick shirt-jacket. They were his work clothes, and I hadn't even noticed since I had been staring at his face.

"I was on the job by six, and I left right when you called. I'm dirty. I washed my hands and dusted off, but I need a shower. I have no clothes, though, Rose. Look at me. Listen to something." Eric looked me straight in the eyes. Those baby blues could absolutely melt me.

"What is it?" I asked, feeling distracted. I wanted to stand on the edge of his eyes and jump into them.

"Rose."

"What?"

"Listen. You need to understand something. I put my phone in my pocket after I got off of the phone with you, and I came here. I told the guys I'd be back tomorrow night, and I got in my truck. I did not stop at my apartment or pack any bags. I literally left the job and came straight here. I'm telling you that because you need to know what you're getting into with me. I am passionate that way, and I don't always think things through. I wanted to get here so fast that I didn't even think about the fact that I would have wished I had showered once I got here."

"I don't care about a shower," I said.

"I'm serious, though, Rose. This is me. This is what you're getting yourself into. I don't know if I'll ever be a normal grown-up human and make good decisions all the time."

"Grown-up humans never make good decisions all the time, Eric. Maybe we need each other. Maybe we can talk each other out of the bad ones."

He took a deep breath. He didn't say anything, but I got the feeling he was relieved that I was still standing there leaning into him. "I really need a shower," he said. "And I didn't even think about needing clothes to change into when I left Arkansas. This is how impulsive I am."

I grinned a little. "I call it passionate. You don't let anyone tell you how to live your life. You just do what you want."

"Thank you for understanding. I do still wish I had some clothes to change into, though."

"I have clothes. I have men's clothes."

Eric started to say something and then he hesitated, making a face like he wasn't quite sure what to think of that.

I laughed. "I have a little area in my closet where I hoard gifts. I know I have a couple of things for my brothers and a few are actually for you. I'm not promising that I can figure out your dream outfit with socks and underwear to match, but I'll hook you up. I can come up with something."

"You're amazing," he said slowly, not taking his eyes off mine.

"You are amazing. I'm speechless. I needed you tonight. I cannot tell you how much I needed you."

"I'm happy you're happy," he said. "Just give me five minutes to shower, and we'll both be happy."

I nodded. "Leave the door unlocked, and I will drop some things in there for you without looking."

"I don't mind if you look," he said, messing with me, smiling that wild-man smile and causing my blood to turn warm.

"I'll leave you some clothes in a pile on the floor by the door," I said, trying not to seem affected.

My world had been turned upside down in a matter of minutes. One second, I was in a melancholy stupor over my mother, and now my world was fine and good. There was simply no way I would let my mother influence me on this one, and Eric's appearance assured me of that.

I went to the bottom of my closet where I had gifts stashed. My brother, AJ, had been wearing various types of food boxers since we were kids. He had collected all sorts of silly cheeseburger, taco, or pizza underwear. I had a pack of three pizza ones from American Eagle, and I ripped into the hanging box, freeing a pair of them. I also had a pair of Adidas sweatpants that were for AJ, and a white sweatshirt that I had bought for Eric.

I made a neatly folded stack of the clothes and opened the door just far enough to slide it onto the bathroom floor. After that, I ran around, cleaning and straightening things.

My heart was full.

I turned on the television to music videos and scrambled around to make the living room inviting for us. Eric had already said he would head back to Arkansas tomorrow. I would only have one night with him. I made my apartment as welcoming as possible—I straightened pictures on the wall and adjusted décor, hiding any laundry that was lying around.

I also ordered food delivery. There was a delicious Thai place not far from my apartment. They were open late, and I knew the menu well. I ordered online so that I wouldn't have to take care of paying for it at the door.

I had just wrapped all of that up when Eric emerged from the bathroom. His hair was wet. He had on the sporty clothes I had left in there for him—the white sweatshirt, with three-stripe pants that fit him like a glove.

I set down my phone, smiling at the sight of him. He held his own clothes in a stack, and he set them on the nearest surface, which was a catch-all table near my hallway.

"These are nice," he said, pinching a piece of fabric from his pants. "I love the shirt, too. It and the pants still had tags, so I took them off, I hope that's okay."

"Yes. And I should've taken them off for you. The boxers are new, too. I took them out of a multi-pack. AJ w-wears food."

"Are these for AJ?" he asked, looking surprised.

"No, no. He doesn't even know I have them."

"I keep a few things in a… I have some candles and everything back there. It's a gift area in my closet."

"You had this whole outfit in a gift area?"

"Yes. The shirt was for you, and I knew it would look amazing on you. White looks so good with your eyes."

"It was for me? When were you planning on giving it to me?"

"I'm not sure actually. I thought about taking it when I went to Arkansas last weekend, but I already had that office stuff for your birthday and I thought it might be too much."

"It is too much, but I'm glad you have it. If you had given it to me then, I wouldn't have it now. Thank you."

I walked over to the couch and flopped onto it. I pulled a nearby blanket onto the couch with me, covering up with it.

"You're welcome. Thank you for being here. We'll have some Thai food in a little while, but for now, I have water and juice and all that in the fridge if you want some."

He nodded and I watched as he went to the fridge and retrieved a bottled water. He drank half of it in one swing and set the other half down. I took a deep breath as I watched him. He made eye contact with me and then jogged over to the couch, diving onto it in a swift, rolling motion.

I readjusted, curling up beside him. He held onto me, snuggling his body close to mine. He smelled clean. He had used my soap, and it smelled different on him than it did on me. He smelled amazing, and I grinned as he wrapped himself around me like a big, muscular anaconda.

"I can't take it," he said. "I can't take being so far. If we're going to figure out a way to be next to each other eventually, then let's do it sooner. I don't feel like being patient."

We didn't look each other in the eyes while he spoke. We snuggled on the couch, Eric wrapping around me and holding me captive. I did not dare move. I didn't want to. I rested my arms around him, relaxing in his embrace.

"I'm glad you're not patient, Eric. I needed you tonight. I need you every night, I think."

"That's what I'm saying," he said, squeezing me.

"I think I'll go to you," I said.

He broke the hold he had on me and looked up, making eye contact with me.

I smiled. "I'll get a job there," I added. "I've been thinking about it all day. I won't be able to find one making what I'm making here, but I won't need that much money."

"No, you don't. I can pay you to work for me," he offered. "I know it's not a dream job, but I would love the help with my books and accounting. I spend about a quarter of my time doing that stuff, and I would love it if that could change. No pressure if you don't want to do that kind of thing, but I—"

"I want to," I said, interrupting him. "I'm nervous about moving there without a plan, and it would make me feel better to have a job possibility."

"I definitely need you at my business," he said "It's up to you whether or not you want to work with me."

"I wonder where I'll live, also."

"I wish with me," he said. "I know we're not doing that until we get married, but what about your uncle until then? I guess I just assumed… I would marry you now. I would do that and have you live with me."

"It might come to that because I'm not sure what my mom will say or if she'll influence my uncle. She likes my job. She likes having me here in Chicago. I feel like she might freak out a little bit if I tell her

I'm moving down there. Especially since Beau's already there. I don't know how many people Uncle Max wants living at his house."

Eric made a face at that. "He wouldn't want you living anywhere else," Eric said reasonably. "Not until you move in with me."

I shrugged. I was feeling so alone before I called him, and the thought of going to him in Arkansas was so glorious that I didn't care about the details.

"It doesn't matter. What I'm saying is that I'm up for whatever. If I have to look for an apartment, I will. I'm not depending on my parents or Uncle Max or anyone. I feel like you—I'm wild, I'm my own woman, nobody's going to tell me what to do. I want to go be with you, and that's what I'm doing. I'm happy when I think about helping you with the business. I think we can do a good job together."

"When are you coming to me, my precious wild one?"

"Soon," I said. "I have to get my things in order here, decide when I want to move, and quit my job." I let my fingertips brush his hairline, smoothing his damp hair. I marveled at the way the hair grew there on his temple, and how the littlest things like that could make me feel attracted to him. "I love everything about you," I said out loud.

He squeezed his body, expertly wrapping around me and holding me in just the right way. He was an athlete and he had body awareness, and he held me and squeezed me and moved with me in his arms causing me to giggle.

We curled up on the couch together and talked until someone knocked on the door. The sound startled me, and Eric sat up and then got to his feet instantly.

"It's takeout," I said, remembering that I had called for food. "Usually, I have to ring them up. I hope they haven't been calling me."

"You're having food delivered?"

"Yes, I told you."

"You said we'd have Thai. I thought you meant we'd cook."

"No. I ordered it while you were in the shower."

I crossed to the door in my pajamas.

"I'll get it," he said. "Let me grab my wallet."

"Oh, I already paid for it," I said. I jogged to the door and opened it just far enough to smile at the delivery man and reach out for the bag. "Thank you," I said, when the guy handed it to me.

He told me he had tried to call me a few minutes ago, and that someone had to let him up. I apologized and thanked him for seeing that the food got to me. I had already given him a generous tip, which was why he was still smiling. I closed the door and turned with the bag in my hands.

"Voila. Delicious, hot, tasty Thai dinner, delivered to our doorstep."

"I had no idea you called that in."

"I did it when you were in the shower. This place really is the best Thai in the city. It's lucky they're right here."

Chapter 18

Eric took off the sweatshirt.

I didn't expect him to do it, but that was the first thing he did when I opened the bag of takeout and took plates out of the cupboard. I saw it happen from the corner of my eye. He stretched upward and took the sweatshirt off over his head before tossing it to the side.

"It's white," he explained when I looked. "I don't want to get anything on it. I'll put it back on when we're finished."

"I probably have a t-shirt in there if you want one… but I'm not complaining," I added, feeling shy and looking down.

"What, you like big muscles or something?" Eric asked, innocently confident.

"I do like your muscles, actually." I cleared my throat, finding it difficult to think of the right words. "Could you possibly get this stuff out of the bag if I run to the restroom and wash my hands? I'll just be a second."

"Of course," he said.

The two of us switched places since I had been standing near the food. I felt flustered. I had seen Eric's bare chest before, but he had definitely been working hard since then, and also, now I was in love with him. I felt suddenly overheated after looking at him, so I went to the restroom. I checked myself in the mirror and decided to brush my teeth.

I had glanced back at Eric as I was on my way to the restroom, and the memory of him in those sweatpants with no shirt was scorched into my mind. I could see it when I blinked. I imagined it as I brushed my teeth. He was literally the perfect man— my perfect man. His chest and shoulders were broad, and he had a thin but muscular athletic frame. He had scars, and I knew what most of them were from. I was hot and bothered by seeing Eric shirtless. He was in my kitchen at this very moment. He was mine, and my body reacted by feeling a rush of heat and excitement.

There was no question in my mind that I was making the right choice. God had sent him here to confirm that. I knew the path I needed to take, and Eric's appearance out of nowhere only solidified everything. I was thinking of him the whole time I was in there absentmindedly brushing my teeth and adjusting my appearance. There had been talk of me uprooting my life and heading to Arkansas in the next couple of weeks, and I was not scared at all. I wasn't freaked out. The only feeling I had was excitement.

I had a flash of my mom, and my stomach turned, but then my next thought was that of Eric. He had been working his butt off to get this business started, and yet he was here with me, letting me know that he was willing to give it all up and start over.

Then I thought of him in those sweatpants. I thought of his bare chest, and I smiled as I washed off my face and dried it. Eric Jones was in my house. The day was so surreal that it didn't have time to sink in properly. But it was real. I had been sitting on the couch with him for almost an hour already. We were making plans to be together long-term. He had said he wanted to come home to me every night. I wanted nothing more than that.

I had some lightly scented lotion in my medicine cabinet, and I put a small amount of it on my arms and stomach before adjusting my hair one last time and heading back out to the living room.

It was just as wonderful as I knew it would be— the sight of him in my kitchen. We weren't at Uncle Max's with everyone around. We were alone, in our own space, and it was just as it should be. I walked over to him and saw that he had two plates prepped and ready to eat.

"This food looks and smells amazing," he said.

I came further into the kitchen and found a place to stand beside him, looking at his work.

"Have you not tasted it?" I asked.

"No, I haven't," he said, turning around. He leaned against the counter and reached out for my hand.

"Why didn't you taste it?" I asked.

"I was waiting for you."

"Oh, I didn't realize," I said, feeling breathless. He stayed where he was, casually resting against the counter, looking me over like a confident alpha male. I felt the need to wiggle. "Thank you for waiting," I added.

Music still played on the TV, and I could hear it in the background, but I could hardly concentrate on anything but the pounding of my own heart. I stood next to him, but not touching him.

"You smell different," he said. "You smell good." He leaned in, sniffing near my neck.

"You surprised me earlier, so I was just in my normal, stinky state."

"You did not stink. Far from it. I love how you smell. This is just something new."

"Yeah, I put lotion on in the bathroom."

I found myself so close to his shirtless body that I could feel his body heat. We had been snuggled up in the cave, and I remembered that moment of being with him, connecting with him in the dark. I couldn't believe this was the body I had been pressed up against.

"I also brushed my teeth," I admitted.

"You brushed your teeth just to come out here and eat Thai food?"

"Not entirely just for that," I said, flirting with him, moving a little closer.

"You went in there and then came out with lotion on and your teeth brushed?" he said, rubbing his jaw and wearing a teasing grin.

"Well, you were asking for it. What am I supposed to do? You're the one out here putting on a gun show."

He laughed and then brought up his arm in a curl position, showing off his biceps, being silly. I reached up and touched his arm, feeling the hard ball of muscle under his skin. My body was on fire for him, and I just smiled and looked casual, taking a deep breath.

"Yeah, see? I have to get all gussied-up after you go flexing that around."

He laughed at me. "I really did just want to keep Thai noodles off of the shirt," he admitted.

"Well, either way, it caused... I, really, I'm feeling all..." I paused and waved my own face as if to cool it off. "Overheated about it."

"Overheated? Are you okay?" He asked the question seriously and slowly, and I could just feel what was about to happen between us.

I stood right next to him, and we could both see the rising and falling of my chest as I breathed. In fact, his chest was moving up and down, too.

I scanned his perfect face. "I'm fine, I'm just... feeling..." I trailed off, not finishing my sentence.

"Feeling what?" he asked slowly.

"Just feeling," I said.

I leaned into him, letting my face brush against his bare chest. Touching him gave me the sensation that I might melt. He used a finger under my chin to ask me to look up.

And then he kissed me. Oh, my goodness, did he kiss me. Eric was a man who knew what he wanted, and what he wanted was me. Goodness, gracious. It was me he wanted. He was gentle but passionate, and I got lost in some kind of ecstasy while he wrapped me in his kiss.

After a minute or two in this paradise, Eric broke the kiss and pulled back. He leaned in and kissed me again just to assure me it was difficult to break away.

"Our food's going to get cold," he said.

I touched the side of his face, knowing that I wanted to spend the rest of my life with him. "It is. We should eat," I said, absentmindedly. "And, I was just thinking about it, and I think we should go ahead and get married," I said. "I mean, will you? Can we? Will you marry me?"

"Yes," he agreed. "Are you asking me, officially, or just mentioning it?"

"I would like to think I'm asking you officially."

"Then, I am saying yes, officially," he said. "I say we make some kind of record of it."

"It's recorded right here," I said. I used my pointer finger and tapped on the side of my head.

"I'm being serious," he said.

"So am I," I agreed.

"If I had a ring I would give it to you right now."

I ran my fingertips down the bare skin of his chest. "If you gave it to me, I would put it on my finger."

"I'm doing that," he said. "I'm buying it. Consider it bought. Let's get online and pick one right now. I don't have much with me, but I do have my debit card. Let's shop right now. Do you need me to get on my knees? Should I?"

"No, you shouldn't," I said, smiling and knowing he would. "I love you. And I'm serious."

"I'm completely serious," he said. "I want to ask you, but I don't know how to do all that stuff girls like. Be honest. I thought you might want me to propose in some special way."

"No, I think right now, over Thai food, is fine," I said, breaking away from him and turning around to pick up a plate. I handed it to him. "The forks are in that drawer," I said, pointing. "There's chopsticks in there, too."

He took the plate from me, but he leaned in and kissed me before the transfer was complete. "When are we doing this?"

"How about by summer?" I said, knowing that was just a few short months away."

"Oh, summer? Oh, well, then, I have time to propose. I thought you were talking about trying to do it really soon so you can just come live with me when you move down."

"Uh, we-well..."

"No, I don't want you to feel pressure to do that, I just thought that's what you were talking about when you asked... if we're waiting till summer, I have time to find a ring and propose. You know, go talk to your dad and everything."

He handed me a fork, and I made a questioning expression at him as I took it. "So that other plan where we get on the computer and get a ring and get engaged tonight, that was the faster version? Getting married soon? Just do it now, and move in with you?"

"Yes, but, Rose, I'm not in a hurry. We don't have to do that."

"Well, I am kind of in a hurry," I said, tilting my head at him.

He grinned. "I need you to know that I care about your dreams," he said.

"Why do you say that?"

"Just because you're moving to Arkansas right now doesn't mean that I've forgotten that you want to work for a big newspaper and live in a bigger city. I want to make that happen for you. I want to make your dreams happen."

"My dreams are happening," I said. "Working for the newspaper was just a plan because I was good at it in college. I will take just as much pleasure helping you build your business as I would doing something like that. And maybe down the road, I can think of a business of my own. But I want to do this with you. And I don't feel like I'm giving anything up. I'm proud of you and how hard you're working. I want to help you."

"What are your parents going to say?" he asked. "Are they going to be disappointed?"

"I don't really care," I said.

"I do," he said, still touching me with his leg even though he was now holding a plate of food.

"I think I would want to do a private wedding, anyway," I said. "Not involve my parents."

"Would they be mad enough that they don't want to be a part of it?" he asked.

"I don't really know," I said. "If we do it soon, they definitely wouldn't understand. They'd try to talk me out of it if they knew I was talking about moving down there in a couple of weeks and doing this."

"But you still want to?" Eric asked. He set down his plate.

"Yes," I said. "No question about it. No doubt in my mind. I don't need or want a big wedding like they want. And they'll see that it all turned out fine once we have a family and a great life."

We both knew we wanted a family. We had talked about it before.

I got a perfect bite of food on my fork, and Eric reached out for my hand, taking it from me and holding it still as he devoured the bite. I squinted at him, pretending I was angry.

"Sorry," he said with his mouth full.

"I'm not mad," I said, getting more food on my fork.

"Oh, it's so good," he moaned.

"I told you. These people are from Thailand."

"Is it going to be weird, going from this to the same four options in Graham Springs?"

"No, it's not," I said. "None of this is weird for me. My parents, and no wedding, choosing a ring online, the same four restaurants… it all sounds like music to my ears. Eric, we're not stuck in Arkansas. We can decide to move any time we want."

"I know, I just want to make sure you're thinking everything through. Usually, I'm the one who makes rash decisions."

"Do you think this decision is rash?"

"No, I don't. I think it's a great decision. I want you to come live with me and marry me. If that's what you want."

"Yes, it's what I want."

"Do you want to plan on it now or in the spring?" he asked.

"I don't know. I think I want to do it sooner, if you want to."

"I'm ready whenever."

Chapter 19

Three weeks later

It was actually happening.

I was moving to Arkansas and marrying Eric Jones. Rose Jones. That would be my new name, and I loved it. The wheels were set in motion, and this was it. I was in my car, headed for my new life, only minutes from my destination.

Eric would be home soon after I got there, and tomorrow we would be married. I wanted to keep the whole thing a huge secret until we had already eloped. I wanted to not tell a soul. But Eric insisted that we inform his parents and a few others in Arkansas. He thought I would ultimately regret it if we did it in complete secrecy.

I did not tell my parents, however. I didn't even tell them I was moving. I talked to my mom this morning while I was driving, and didn't say a thing to her. I cried afterward. I hated lying to her, and leaving Chicago without her knowing felt terrible. I had to do it, though. I was going to marry Eric, and if my mother knew about it. she would try to put a stop to it. She would try to sabotage it. There was just no way I could tell her. I was looking forward to calling her once it was said and done, though. I would cry and tell her that I would miss her and she would forgive me and say that she loved me and would see me soon when she came to Arkansas to visit. Ultimately, I wanted her approval, and I couldn't wait until all this was behind us and she could cool down and forgive me.

It hurt me to have to sneak around behind my family's back. But it didn't hurt enough to change plans. The pain of not being with Eric would be worse than what I felt now, so I chose the lesser pain. Maybe that was selfish of me. Maybe it was wrong of me to choose love over family. I thought it was my mother who was wrong for forcing me to make that choice in the first place.

I had to shake those feelings, though.

I would be seeing my love momentarily. He wanted to be at his apartment when I arrived, but I juked him and didn't call from the road. I planned to get here and freshen up for him.

I had sent an entire storage unit ahead of me, and now I was pulling into town with the last of my belongings packed into my car. I had always flown to Arkansas in the past, and it felt odd to roll up there in my vehicle. It was a dreamlike feeling. I thought things were already overwhelming, but it all began to escalate when I pulled up at his place and saw my uncle Max's SUV parked out front.

I wasn't sure if he knew I was coming.

I knew what to expect at Eric's apartment, and this was not it. This was a couple's home, and there was no mistaking the blacked-out SUV in the driveway. It belonged to Max. I parked beside it and got out of my car, staring into the vehicle even though I couldn't see a thing. Eric's truck wasn't here. I knew he wouldn't be here. He had left a key outside for me in case I beat him here.

The passenger's window came down.

It wasn't Max in the car.

It was my mother, sitting in the passenger's seat. My father was there, too. He was driving.

My stomach turned, and I thought I might be sick.

Astrid and Danny.

I suddenly felt like I was eight years old—like I was running away from home with a blankey and a stuffed animal, and I had been caught.

I fought against those emotions, keeping my face calm. I turned my car off so I could hear them, but I didn't get out or even open the door.

"Eric knows we're here," my mom said, first thing. "He doesn't know we're at his house. He thinks you're meeting us for dinner tonight."

"What's going on, Mom?" I asked, seriously.

I felt like I had been betrayed, and I wanted to start the car, put it in reverse, and leave.

"Come on, Rose, we've been sitting here for over an hour waiting for you. A few weeks ago, Eric showed up at our house. He wrote a letter to us. Would you please just get into the car so I don't have to yell?"

"I'm not getting in the car with you," I said, thinking she was trying to take me away from Eric.

"Please," she said. "I know you're planning on moving here. I'm not trying to stop you."

"You're not?"

"No, just get in the truck with us, Rose. We're here for you."

I did as she asked. I was reluctant about it, but this was my family and there was no way I could run away from this confrontation. I sat in the backseat.

"Where are we going?" I asked when my dad started backing out of the driveway.

"Driving," my mom said decisively.

My dad took off, going down the road, and my mom repositioned, looking at me from the front seat. She took a long, hard look at me, and I just sat there, not giving her anything, waiting to hear what she would say.

"Eric came to us a few weeks ago. He came to our home one morning, saying he had just left you. He had written a letter, telling us everything and explaining his intentions. Your father and I sat there and read it right in front of him. We ended up talking to him for a long time after that. He stayed for two hours."

"What?"

My dad was nodding.

"In Chicago?" I asked.

"Yes," my mom said.

"We talked to him for a long time, and could see his love for you and his intentions for you," Dad said.

"He's a very sincere young man," Mom added. "He told us all about your plans—that you were coming here, and that you plan to get married right when you arrive."

"Tomorrow, yes."

"And you were just going to do it without us?" Dad asked.

"You guys didn't give me much of a choice."

"I guess I deserve that, Rose."

We rode for a minute in silence, all of us thinking.

"Eric told us about his place," Dad said, finally.

"Yes, he did," Mom agreed. "And we came over yesterday and saw it. He said you'd be moving into his apartment for a few months until you get a job and find something else."

"That's the plan," I said.

"We like him," Mom said. "We put together a wedding at uncle Max's tomorrow. I didn't want you to know about it. Eric thinks we're going to surprise you tonight at dinner and tell you all about your wedding plans. But now I'm telling you something he doesn't know. Your father and I want to give the two of you our blessing. We have money set aside for your wedding, Rose. We bought a few things for tomorrow, but we spent no more than a couple of thousand for everything. Uncle Max built a... well, you'll see. But anyway, we didn't spend that much putting everything together for tomorrow. Either way, though, Rose, your father and I have money set aside for you, and we've decided to give it to you a different way. You're under contract. It's under Eric's name and yours, but we won't close for a couple of weeks."

"What, Mom?" I asked, realizing she was using home-buying jargon.

"That's where we're taking you now," she said. "We'll pay the down payment, and enough of your principal where your note should be manageable on this place. Real estate's always a good investment, so you'll get the money back when you go to sell it."

"Uncle Max had a woman who helped us with it," Dad said.

"A good realtor," Mom added. "She's got impeccable taste."

"The current owners are still living in it, so we can't go inside, but there she is…" Dad motioned out of the window proudly.

I glanced that way and saw that there was a house with a sign out front that clearly said it was pending. It was an adorable place situated on lakefront property.

"It's not a mansion," Mom warned.

"It's amazing!" I said, looking out of the window.

"It's a three bedroom, two bath. Go a little faster, Danny. They're home and they're going to catch us looking. It's the third time we've driven by here today."

My dad continued driving by the home as I craned my neck to take in every last detail. I couldn't believe it. It was my own little lakeside cottage. There were neighbors, but there were also woods, and we had plenty of privacy. My heart was beating like crazy as I stared over my shoulder at the house.

"I don't know what to say," I said, staring out of the back of the truck.

"You can thank Eric," my mom said. "He convinced us, Rose. He's a good young man with a good heart, and he seems to really love you. We wanted to help you guys out—get you started. If you are going to choose to be here, we wanted to help you get the best start possible."

I watched out of the back window as we drove away from the house.

"We close in two weeks," Mom said. "And the realtor is going to get you an appointment to go over there sometime before that, but we can't just drop in on them."

"I am speechless, you guys. I'm tired from driving and today has been kind of surreal leaving Chicago, so seeing you here and having you say this it's just un-be-liev-a-ble."

I didn't even realize I was crying.

There were just silent rivers of tears flowing down my cheeks before I knew it. I leaned against the backseat, sinking down and hiding my face.

Relief. Sweet relief. It wasn't about the money or the house. It was my parents' approval. I had been playing it cool with Eric but I had been secretly craving it. It was such a relief to have their approval that I just sat back and cried.

"What in the world, Rose?" my mom questioned, glancing back and seeing me bawl.

"I'm happy," I said, sitting up and trying to stop crying. "I'm seriously just happy. That's what this is about."

"Eric knows we're here, but he knows nothing about the house. We did that behind his back. We were planning on giving him that at the wedding."

"What are we talking as far as a wedding goes?" I asked.

"Fifty or sixty people. Eric has some friends and family coming and we have about twenty on our side. Your brothers are here. More wanted to be here, but it was short notice. Uncle Don's working, but Aunt Sarah's here, Max, Casey, Charlie and Hope, of course. It might be a few more than fifty, but it's not a big deal. We got some catering from a place in Little Rock. We'll have a ten-minute ceremony and share a meal together. Don't cry. Rose, stop."

My mom began opening compartments, looking for tissues. She gave me a stack of fast food napkins out of the console, and I hid my face and wiped my eyes with them.

"While we're at it, we should also tell you that we got you a honeymoon."

"You're kidding me."

"I'm not. It's nothing fancy, nothing overseas—we just got you a nice place down in Florida, the Keys. You'll spend next week there."

"Next week?"

"Yes, five days because I know how Eric works. That just leaves you one week in his apartment before your new place is ready."

I took a deep breath.

"We love you, Rose, and we planned for you to experience these things. It would be wrong of us to take that away from you just because Eric is... Eric is actually great," she said, stopping herself. "And he doesn't know about the trip or the house."

"No, he doesn't," Dad added. "We're going to tell you that tonight at dinner."

My mom sighed. "Rose, I just want to make sure that you're not doing things this fast because of me and our disapproval. If you want to wait to get married, I'll still support you. Just because we're planning on doing it tomorrow doesn't mean we have to. Nobody will care if we—"

"I want to marry Eric for no other reason than wanting to marry him."

"This fast?" Mom asked, trying not to judge, but truly wondering.

"Yes, this fast. This doesn't seem fast to me. I've loved him a long time."

My mom turned around in her seat and was quiet after that because she knew I was telling the truth. "Well, I'm sorry for pushing what I wanted on you," she said.

I thought she was going to say more, but she left it at that. It was a rare thing for her to apologize.

"Thank you, Mom. Thank you for saying that. I'm glad you and Dad are here, and I'm so happy you worked things out with Eric. I don't even care what you have planned for tomorrow, I'm just relieved that you're here."

Chapter 20

My parents dropped me off at Eric's, and I spent the next few minutes showering and getting ready for him to get off work. I had packed and been on the road all day and I felt like I needed to do that. Thank goodness I had a minute alone because the thing with my parents was a lot to take in.

I was in the apartment for about a half-hour before I talked to Eric. During that time alone, my emotions went from happiness to regret, relief, fear, and eight or ten other things. I left my whole life behind today, and the whole time I had this cloud hanging over me about my parents. The relief I felt from their approval was like a literal weight off my shoulders. I felt like I could physically stand taller.

And then I realized that Eric had known this whole time. He didn't know how nervous I was about my parents or he would have reassured me and told me they knew. I could see now that everything I had been so torn up about had never even come to pass.

I thought about all those things and let the things my parents had told me sink in during that time alone. I washed my face with cold water since I had cried, and I was clean and better suited to face the evening by the time I finished my shower.

I had a missed call from Eric when I was in there, and I called him back as soon as I got out.

"Hey," I said, when I heard him pick up.

"Where are you?" he asked.

"I'm here. I got here a little while ago."

"You're kidding. I thought you were going to call me from the road."

His voice. I talked to him all the time, but I hadn't seen him in three weeks, and the sound of his voice was different now that I knew I would be seeing him in a little while. I began to feel those familiar butterflies, and I felt an urgent need to get my hair out of a towel.

"Where are you?" I added as I walked quickly back to the bathroom.

"I'm on my way home."

"Really?"

"Yes. I'll be there in ten minutes."

Those ten minutes were the fastest of my life. Not only did I have to get my own appearance in order, but I wanted to clean up the mess I had made when I came in and brought some things out of my car.

Eric was a neat and tidy person, so my trail of things had been obvious. I cleaned up and got myself fixed up, and the next thing I knew, I heard his truck pull into the driveway.

I went to the front door and opened it. The truck stopped moving, the engine turned off, and there was nothing I could do to stop myself from going to him.

I rushed to Eric, jogging as fast as my feet could take me.

He scrambled to get out of the truck in time to catch me in his arms. He laughed and nestled his face into my neck kissing me.

We stopped moving and he set me on my feet.

"I'm so happy you're here," he said, his eyes sparkling. "I can't believe it. I'm about to marry you tomorrow. I need to take you on a honeymoon. We need to plan something this spring—maybe somewhere tropical?"

"Hmm, how about Florida?" I asked.

I held his hand as we walked inside, and I felt a current of warm electricity emanating from the place where we touched. Eric was exactly the man I desired, and he was mine. I could not believe this was my life. I would live anywhere as long as it was with him.

"Florida? Not just Florida—somewhere overseas maybe. Can we afford that yet? I think we can."

I pulled him inside and we closed the door. "I think Florida's great," I said.

"Yeah, you're right. I just wanted to go as far away with you as I can—take you to the edge of the world to show you off."

I laughed. "The Florida Keys *are* the edge of the world."

"Is that where you want to go? The Florida Keys? I think I could manage that. Speaking of a honeymoon, I need to talk to you about wedding stuff. I have a gigantic, non-material surprise for you tonight, and I want to go ahead and tell you about it so that you can prepare yourself. It's really big news."

"Prepare myself?"

"It's your mom," he said.

"She's here," I said with a nod.

"What? You know?"

"Yes, I do," I said, cracking a smile at his surprise. He was so irresistible that I hugged him again.

"I need a shower," he said, pulling back.

"Nu-uh," I protested, drawing closer to him.

"You knew about your mom?" he asked, looking confused.

"Just now," I said. "I got here a little while ago, and she and my dad were sitting in the driveway."

"Really? How'd they know?"

I shook my head.

"I'm sorry they did that," he said. "We were supposed to surprise you tonight, and I've held my tongue until now, but I was about to tell you. I wanted to save you from being blindsided, but I guess you were blindsided anyway. I'm sorry if you're upset I didn't tell you sooner. We were trying to make it a surprise for you. Your mom had wanted to do that."

"Well, they have some other surprises, too, but they told me about them, and now I'm going to tell you."

He raised his eyebrows. "What do you mean?" he asked.

"Big stuff," I said.

"I love you," he said.

"Don't you want to hear about the big stuff?"

"Yeah, but I love you. I want you to know that I love you and I'm happy you're here. It's just me and you, okay?"

He wrapped his arms around me, and I nodded. "It is just me and you. And my parents got us a trip to Florida. It's the Keys. They planned it. I think they talked to Billy and Zack about your jobs coming up. I think they've done some things to work it out for us. But it's a honeymoon. Next week."

"Next week?"

I nodded. "I think we leave soon."

He smiled and looked me over. "That's a good secret. I love that secret. Did your parents pay for it? If so, that was really nice. Is that what your mom told you when they came over here? What all did they say?"

I smiled. "Well, first I had to get over the shock of seeing them. They told me you came and saw them and brought a letter."

"I did. Right after I left you that day. I wrote it in a Target parking lot. I stopped and bought a notebook. And your mom told me that same day that she wanted to make all of this a surprise, otherwise I would've told you."

"In hindsight, I probably had hints. I just didn't pick up on any of them."

"I was really trying to keep it a secret for your mom. I was about to tell you, though."

"I'm glad because it might have been a shock to see her tonight. Are others eating dinner with us tonight?"

"Yes. I think like twenty or so. Your family and a few of my people. It's at that burger place. Tomorrow's going to be at Max's and fairly low-key, except for my friend, Alan, told me that your uncle was building a really nice halfpipe at his house. Actually, I know it's true. Alan's brother-in-law was out at the property working on it last week. He said it's great. Anyway, they built this whole thing and we're gonna hang out and get to use it after the wedding."

"That's amazing," I said. "A ramp?"

"Yes, and it's big. I'm excited to see it, and a couple of my friends who know how to skate well are coming, so it should be fun. No one knows I know about it. Max told the crew not to mention it to anyone, but you know how word spreads. It was supposed to be a secret."

"Okay, now I'm struggling a little bit to keep up," I said.

"Why? Was that too much information with the halfpipe thing?"

"I'm not even sure what to imagine."

"It's a gigantic ramp. An amazing skate ramp that's about ten feet tall and twenty feet long—it's got a ramp on both sides—like a half of a pipe."

"I've seen those. He did that?"

Eric nodded. "Alan said it's nice. And why is it too much information?" he asked.

"No, it's not too much usually, it's just that's not even all of the surprises. I still have one to tell you and it's definitely the biggest one."

"This is a twenty-foot wooden structure in his yard. It's like bigger than this whole apartment."

"What I'm talking about is still bigger news than this."

"What in the world?"

"Another gift from my parents. Help with a house, Eric. It's a down payment and then some, and it's adorable. I am so happy. I can't wait to show you. Wait. I don't even think I know the address. I'd take you now, but I don't know how to get there."

"Whoa, whoa, whoa, slow down. A house?"

"Yes. They bought it right after you talked to them. They didn't pay for the whole thing, but I think the down payment was significant enough that we can be comfortable with the mortgage. It's not a mansion or anything, but it's really adorable."

He stared at me. "I'm stunned. I can't believe your parents did that."

"They really like you. They said it was money they set aside for my wedding, anyway. I think Uncle Max knew a realtor who found this place before it went on the market. We close in two weeks, and one of those weeks will be spent in Florida."

"Wait, I already forgot Florida was a thing," he said, having a hard time keeping up.

"See, I told you. So many surprises. It's hard to keep them straight."

"Do I need to act surprised about the house, the trip, or both?" he asked.

"Both."

"I'll act surprised, all around," he said with a nod. "The wedding is at six tomorrow. Remember, neither of us are supposed to know about the skate bowl."

I smiled. "I'll pretend I don't know anything."

"I'm taking a shower," he said. He leaned in and kissed me on the lips and then pulled away.

"Could you please wear that same white sweatshirt so you can take it off when we eat dinner?" I asked.

"You want me to eat a big, bare-chested dinner with our friends and loved ones at the restaurant?"

I laughed. "I already forgot we were eating with everyone tonight. Maybe, on second thought, you can keep your shirt on for that."

"I'll tell you when I'm going to take it off is right now," he said, pulling his work shirt off as he backed up, heading for the shower. I watched in awe as he finished the maneuver. He definitely knew what he was doing. He wanted me to look and he smiled at me for doing it.

"Did they really get us a house?"

"Yes, not fully, but yes. We sign papers in two weeks. I think they need our signature this weekend. And it's so sweet—the house, I mean. It's on the lake, Eric."

"You saw it?" he asked, peeking his head around the corner.

"Yes."

"A picture, or with your own eyes?"

"We drove by there. I saw it. I'm going to live there with you."

Eric shook his head in disbelief and then he turned and disappeared into the bathroom, hitting the top of the door jamb on his way inside in a celebratory gesture. "I'll be out in five minutes," he yelled.

Epilogue

The following evening

We did it.

We were married.

I was officially Mrs. Eric Jones. It hadn't quite sunk in yet. Eric and I said some short, sweet vows and then we both said the words 'I do' in front of our families and about thirty of Eric's friends. It was a fun, casual party that Eric and I got all dressed up for, and I thought it was the best wedding ever.

We had the ceremony and ate together, and now we were all hanging out. There were heaters outside in the patio area, and that was where everything was set up. It was hilarious to me that Uncle Max had built a halfpipe. He said he had never seen Eric and his friends skate on a proper ramp, and he wanted to surprise him with it. He would have it taken down after a little while, but it was such a sweet gesture.

The ramp itself was steep, and there was no way I was going down it in roller skates, but Eric loved skating on it, and he was good. He and his friends had already been on it for a while. It was fun to watch and we had gotten some pretty great wedding photos that featured it.

Eric had been so focused on his job lately that it was fun for me to see him cutting up on his skateboard again. He had gotten dressed up for the wedding, but in the couple of hours since then, he unbuttoned the collar of his shirt and rolled his cuffs, making his dressy attire skateboard friendly.

He was irresistible.

There was music, and it felt like a fun summer get-together in the dead of winter. We could have never gotten away with this in Chicago.

I had come inside a few minutes ago to take some dishes to the kitchen, and it seemed that in those brief moments when I wasn't looking at Eric, he had managed to go and get hurt.

He was smiling as he came my way, but I could see a scrape on the side of his face. "What did you do?" I asked.

"It's really nothing," he said. "I just came in to wash off."

"Come in here with me."

I met him on the other side of the kitchen, and we headed down the hall, toward a small half-bath. A few others came into the kitchen as we walked out, and we could hear them, but they couldn't see us now that we had made our way toward the restroom.

Eric was in front of me as we walked, and I stared at him. I loved how he walked, the way he took a stride. I loved how he looked in those pants. I stared unabashedly at his body. I had wanted him for so long that this day was completely unbelievable.

"Rose Jones, I've wanted to be that for so long," I said quietly when the thought crossed my mind.

Eric glanced back at me when I said it. He stopped in the doorway of that tiny restroom, turning to me. I stared at his perfect face. He had a scrape on the top of his cheek, near the side of his eye… several red streaks lightly pierced the skin and I sucked air through my teeth when I inspected it. My reaction caused Eric to glance inside the bathroom, trying to look at himself in the mirror.

"That's nothing," he said smiling and reassuring me. "I didn't even know that was there. This is what I was washing off."

He held up his elbow and I gasped when I saw the amount of blood.

"It's nothing also," he said. "I just knew my shirt was white, and…. " He trailed off as he unbuttoned his shirt.

"I'll run and get you a shirt to change into," I said, taking off down the hallway.

By the time I got back with a clean shirt, Eric had his wound tended to and everything put back in order.

"Thank you," he said. "See? It's no big deal." Before he put the shirt on he turned his arm so that I could see his elbow. There was a bandage on it, and it was clean and no longer bleeding. "Thank you for this," he said. "I washed my face, too, and it's nothing, see?"

He turned, but I could still see the small scrape mark. It was masculine and rugged, and I could not get enough of how he looked.

"You have to be more careful on that ramp," I said, getting closer to him, flirting. "I don't like to see you bleeding."

"I'm not going to do it all the time, I just did it tonight because I was showing off."

"Who were you showing off for? I wasn't even out there."

"I wanted you to hear tales of my glory. I haven't skated in a while, so I didn't want you to see me have a close call if I tried something complicated."

I squinted my eyes playfully at him. "I'm sorry you fell," I said.

"It wasn't bad at all," he said. "And at least I landed the trick."

"I'm sort of glad I didn't watch," I said.

"You don't want to see how bad I am on a ramp?" (The word bad in that question meant good, and I knew it.) I could tell by the way he was staring straight at me with confidence.

"I am pretty sure I already think you're bad. I don't know why I said bad right there. I don't normally say that, and it came out weird. I was too busy staring at your mouth. I was distracted, but it was your own fault. I can't talk right."

"You're too busy staring at my mouth to think straight? Is that what you just said?"

He stared at me like he couldn't believe I would say such a thing. He made a serious face, but I knew he was joking around, because he licked his lips. My core felt suddenly warm, and my body did not take it as a joke.

"I can't believe we leave for Florida in two days," I said.

"I can't think of anything beyond tonight." He had his new shirt on, and he pulled me into his arms, looking like he was a predator and I was his prey. I had to stifle a giggle.

"Where's Eric?" we heard someone ask.

The voices sounded like they were closer to our side of the kitchen now.

"I think he went to see about his elbow."

"More like swellbo. I can't believe he landed that. What was it?"

I looked at him, and he shrugged innocently.

"I don't know, I didn't see it," someone else said.

"I think that dude, Casey, got it on video."

"It was a kickflip and something else, and he landed it, he ran out of room, so he just had to slide and roll afterward. He landed it, though."

"Dude hasn't skated in a year. He's been swinging a hammer for ten hours a day, and now he's over here going insane on that halfpipe."

We heard them say something else about Eric and then start laughing.

I made eye contact with Eric again, and he stretched his mouth downward in just the right way to say he was sorry.

"I'm not trying to hurt myself," he whispered, explaining. "I was just giving the people what they wanted since your uncle went through all the trouble of putting up the ramp. I didn't think there would be blood."

I grinned at him. "Don't you already know? I love it that you're wild."

Eric's hand came around my lower back, and he pulled me toward him, staring at me with that same predatorial, challenging stare. He kissed me gently, letting his warm, soft, sticky, perfect mouth rest on mine for a glorious gut-wrenching second before slowly pulling back. His blue eyes stared into mine.

"Guess what, Rose?"

"What?"

"You're the wild one for being with me."

I grinned. "I love you."

"I know," he said.

"Good."

"I love you, too," he added.

"I know," I said.

He smiled. "Good."

The End

(till book 6)

Thanks to my team ~ Chris, Coda, Skye, Jan, Glenda, and Yvette